INFECTED CITY BOOK 1:

EMERGENCY BROADCAST

BORIS BACIC

Contents

FOREWORD

A word of warning. This book is a departure from what I usually write. For years now, I've had an itch to write a book about zombies, but I kept putting it off because my passion was directed at other projects.

Still, this story deserved to be published as a book of its own because of how far it helped me come.

Back when I was still an avid reader of Creepypasta and Nosleep stories, something had awoken inside me— an itch to put words on paper. I wrote short stories for my own pleasure and posted them on Reddit. I would look at all those other stories getting thousands of upvotes while mine got a measly fifty or sixty, and I would wonder what they did to be so good.

It was frustrating because it hit my ego and told me I wasn't good enough to write. So, I wrote "Emergency Broadcast," a one-part short story, and I said to myself, if this story doesn't get any attention, I'm throwing in the towel.

When I woke up, my phone exploded with notifications of comments asking me to give them an update on the story. I wrote the next part, which was even more popular. It ended up being five parts, and the comments had nothing but good things to say about it.

That was how my career as a writer started.

Looking back, it was very wrong of me to measure how good of a writer I am based on the number of upvotes. Since writing "Emergency Broadcast," I had posted stories that garnered thousands of upvotes that I personally thought was drivel, and there were those that got barely a few hundred, which went on to become very successful books.

The point I'm trying to make here is: If you're an artist of any kind, don't worry about the number of likes, views, and upvotes. Keep posting or sharing things that mean to you even if only one person sees them.

Do it for you.

HEATHER

Baldwin River was one of the first neighborhoods to be hit by the outbreak in Witherton. It wasn't enough that it took first prize for being the poorest and most dangerous place in the city. It also had to nab first place in being overrun by the red-eyed people.

Red-eyed people. That was what Abby called them the first time they saw them on the news, and the moniker stayed, because it was fairly simple, and the news had no official name for them.

It started shortly after Heather came back from work as a waitress at the Wonder Meal diner. On her drive back, the radio in the car spoke about strange occurrences inside the city and people going crazy and violently attacking others—in Baldwin River, of course, because where else would it happen?

It wasn't mentioned, but Heather assumed drugs were involved—either excess usage or lack of. She turned off the radio when the person on the news advised the residents of Baldwin River to be careful. It was clear that the speaker never stepped into the neighborhood. Otherwise, he'd know that being careful was a daily routine there.

Heather wasn't worried about the news at the time. Every now and again, news like that erupted from Baldwin, and a person living there could only have so many scares before realizing the media vastly exaggerated happenings in the city, especially in Baldwin.

But when she arrived at the apartment complex, the scene that unfolded before her eyes convinced her that this might not be an ordinary news scare.

A car had crashed into the wall just across the street. It was so loud Heather initially thought it was a gunshot. The front of the car was totaled, and when the door opened, a man stepped outside and started running down the street while screaming.

The scariest thing about the whole thing?

He was running with an open fracture on his leg.

Seeing it happen right in front of the apartment where she lived with her sister made unease bloom inside her. Sure, she heard about these things on the news all the time, but she never actually saw it happening. It was like seeing something you already knew in theory presented in practice for the first time.

Abby had been thrilled when Heather returned home because the two of them were supposed to go to the park. Heather hated having to topple Abby's hopes, but she felt that it would be safer to stay inside until the situation calmed down.

Except, it didn't calm down like she hoped it would. Baldwin grew more restless and violent. Distant gunshots and screams became a daily occurrence. The sound circled the building where Heather and Abby lived, drawing nearer and farther like a shark surrounding its prey.

Until a gunshot ripped inside the apartment right above theirs. There had been yelling and things breaking, which Heather could hear clearly because of the thin walls in the building. Then came the gunshot, and it was so loud it made Heather jump and Abby cry.

Heather called the police, and they said they would send someone to check it out. No one ever came, but the commotion upstairs stopped along with the gunshot.

Baldwin had practically become a war zone. People were dying daily, and the news about people going crazy refused to abate. The plague of violent attacks was not constrained only to Baldwin River, either. Soon, news articles popped up about attacks all over Witherton.

It was Heather's two days off, and she already dreaded driving back to work and leaving Abby alone at home. Then came the emergency alert sent to her phone just an hour before her shift at the diner.

Lock your doors, cover your windows, and avoid making too much noise. Do not go outside under any circumstances. You will receive further instructions soon.

"Shit," Heather said for multiple reasons.

She'd skip work, which meant less money. But more worrisome was the fact that she'd received an emergency alert text in the first place because it confirmed what she feared all along—this was all real, and it was serious enough for the government to have to warn the citizens.

Heather called Dwayne, her boss, to let him know what was going on. He picked up on the fifth ring.

"Yeah?" he asked.

"Dwayne, it's Heather. Listen, something weird is going on in the city. I just got a government alert."

She waited to see if he would confirm that, yes, he got it, too, and he understood how dangerous it was to be outside.

The pause told her he had no idea what she was talking about. "Alert? What kind of an alert?"

Did he not watch the news and see what a mess the city was in? Dwayne lived in Bryant, so he probably didn't care as long as he had his own peace and quiet. He had no idea how bad things were in Baldwin.

"They're telling us to stay inside," Heather said. "Something going on out there."

"Uh-huh," Dwayne said.

He wasn't getting her point. She didn't call him to share the fun fact that she got an emergency message.

"So, considering that everything's so messed up right now, are you going to close the diner, or…?" she asked.

"Uh, no. I don't see a reason to do that." Dwayne sounded close to offended.

I just told you the reason.

"Okay, my shift starts in less than an hour, and I just received this text, so…"

"Uh-huh. So, are you going to make it to work?"

He really wasn't making things easy for her.

"Like I said, they're telling us to stay inside, so no."

"Sis! Sis!" Abby shouted from the other room.

"Not now, Abby. Anyway, as I was saying, they're telling us not to go outside."

"I see. What did you say the reason was?" Dwayne asked.

Heather closed her eyes for a moment, trying not to lose her temper. "There's something going on out there. People are killing each other, they're—"

"Heather!" Abby called out.

Heather muted her phone and shouted, "Abby, I'm on the damn phone!" She unmuted herself. "Sorry, it was my sister."

"Cool. How's she doing?"

"She's fine," Heather said, even though she really didn't want to talk about Abby right then.

"So, you said people are, what? Killing each other out there?" Dwayne asked.

"Yes."

"Heather, people are killing each other every day. If I closed down the diner every time someone died…"

"But this isn't just someone dying, Dwayne. Why else would I receive an emergency text telling me to stay inside?"

"I didn't receive anything. Are you sure it's not spam?"

It was perhaps Dwayne's calm manner of speaking that got Heather so angry.

"Sis! Sis!" Abby shouted again from the other room.

Heather muted herself once more, her jaw clenched in anger. "Abby, I swear to fucking God, if you don't let me finish this phone call in peace, we're not going to the park for a week!"

She didn't mean to swear, but she lost her temper. It happened often. Living with a seven-year-old child that had autism tended to cause such outbursts.

"Hello? Are you still there?" Dwayne's voice came from the other end when she raised the phone back to her ear.

"Yeah. Sorry about that."

"Okay, well, listen, Heather. You're calling me less than an hour before your shift starts to tell me you won't be able to make it. That's unprofessional of you."

Is he being serious right now?

"Um, I called you as soon as I received the alert," she said.

Why was she even justifying herself to this asshole? He didn't care about his employees.

Because you need the job, she reminded herself.

As much as she hated working at Wonder Meal, it paid the bills.

"That's still no excuse," Dwayne said. "Now I'll have to find someone who can cover for you, and that's gonna come out of your paycheck."

Great.

"Dwayne, it's not my fault," she said. "I'm just doing what the government is advising us to do. I'm not going to risk my life because you think the alert was fake. Just turn on the news, and—"

But Heather was once again interrupted by Abby calling to her. That was the final drop in an already overflowing glass. She stamped into the foyer, not bothering to mute herself this time.

"Abby, how many times do I have to tell you to—"

But once she entered, she stopped yelling because she knew right away that something was off. Abby stood a few feet from the door, her gaze sheepishly stuck to the floor.

A huff came from the other side of the door, followed by a receding patter of footsteps. That paled in comparison to the blood under the door.

Heather's first thought was that Abby was hurt, but upon giving her a once-over, she saw no injuries. That could have only meant one thing, then.

Heather raised the phone to her ear. She ignored Dwayne's babbling about work ethics and said, "I'm gonna have to call you back."

Dwayne went mute for a moment. "Wait, what? You can't just—"

But Heather had already hung up on him. She approached Abby and gently put a hand on her shoulder. "Abby? Are you okay?"

But Abby wasn't responding. She was staring at the pool of blood that seeped into the foyer, hyperventilating.

"It's okay," Heather said. "It'll be okay."

The look of anxiety seemed to diminish from Abby's face until a bang exploded on the door. Both sisters jumped back, and Abby screamed.

"Shh, shh, it's fine. You're fine," Heather said. "Why don't you go to the living room and get that puzzle out you like? We can play that. Okay?"

Abby nodded fervently then walked into the living room with small, timid steps.

"I'll be there in a minute, Sis," Heather said.

Her phone started ringing in her hand. It was Dwayne. She declined the call and muted her phone. She looked down at the blood under the door. It was quickly drying.

Heather approached the door with bated breath, making sure to step around the pool of blood. It was probably her imagination, but she thought she detected a faint, metallic whiff.

"I have the puzzle ready, Sis!" Abby shouted from the living room.

Her voice no longer sounded distraught.

"Okay! I'll be there in a minute!" Heather said.

She peeked through the peephole and gasped just when her phone vibrated.

The wall in front of the apartment was covered in an abundance of blood. Heather vaguely became aware that her fingers were fumbling with the lock, even though the door was already locked. She'd kept it that way ever since she last returned from work, and she and Abby hadn't left the apartment since.

She stepped away from the door, heart thudding in her chest. Her phone vibrated again. She wanted to chuck it against the wall. She unlocked it to see two messages from Dwayne.

This is extremely unprofessional of you, Heather. You can expect a deduction in your salary this month.

Call Tracy and tell her she'll be covering for you tonight.

It was supposed to be Dwayne's job to find a replacement, not Heather's. What if Heather had an emergency and couldn't use her phone?

But, of course, Dwayne would let Heather handle that. He blamed Heather for not being able to make it to work; thus it was her job to make amends. Also, nobody wanted to call a single mother to tell her to cancel her plans with her son so she could go to work.

"Sis?" Abby called.

"Just…" She was about to snap but managed to contain her anger. "Just give me a second, okay?"

She went into her messages with Tracy and typed, *We have an emergency in the neighborhood. Government says not to leave homes. Can't make it to work, and Dwayne insists on keeping the diner open. Can you cover for me?*

As soon as she hit send, she shoved the phone into her pocket and raised a hand to her forehead. Her fingers were icy. She needed a minute to compose herself.

She returned to the living room and sat on the floor in front of Abby, the puzzle depicting dinosaurs splayed in pieces between them. Abby was saying something related to the puzzle, but Heather couldn't focus.

All she could think about was how long they would need to wait for the neighborhood to be safe again.

JAMES

It was James's day off work that Thursday. He hadn't planned on doing anything spectacular. He'd spent the last few months working so much overtime for his company that he could physically feel his health deteriorating.

It was small things at first: a constant feeling of sleepiness, exhaustion, and a lack of motivation for physical exercising. A few months into the project, the situation worsened: focus difficulties, a fever that was just looming above him, waiting for him to skip his daily dose of C vitamins, etcetera.

James had been determined to push through this project to the end because he was hoping for a raise. But yesterday, two days after the project was finished, James texted his manager, asking if he was going to get that promised raise or if he should use up his PTO.

I don't see room for a raise right now, the manager had responded to him, to which James replied by booking two days of PTO. With the weekend, that would account for four days off, which was more than he'd had in a long time.

He could tell what a great idea the days off were the moment he woke up rested without a blaring alarm to startle him out of bed. It was 10 a.m. when he got up to make breakfast, and he spent the next few hours lying on his bed and scrolling through social media.

By afternoon, he was starting to think that all the piled damages that he'd done to himself with overworking were slowly dispersing with just this one day off of work. He was happy with his role in his company; he just wished that he had better time management.

When lunchtime came—which was always around 2 p.m.—James opened the fridge to see what he could cook. The measly stick of butter and half-finished pudding that greeted him from the interior reminded him of how much he relied on the company's free food daily.

That was okay. At least, now he had an excuse to go outside and do some grocery shopping. His phone produced a loud ping the moment he scooped it off the couch. It was a text from Julie, and that immediately brought a smile to James's face.

Heyyyy. How's it going? I'm slacking here with my draft, by the way!!

James let out a chuckle.

Hello there, he responded. **I actually took a day off. Going to do some grocery shopping and try to make lunch. If I stop responding, it means the food killed me.**

Julie's response came moments later. **LOL. You didn't strike me as someone who ever took days off. I need to take a day off and go to the beach, but I don't think I'd be comfortable leaving my apartment by myself, especially with what happened last night.**

What happened last night?

You didn't see the news?

No, what happened?

Witherton's a small town. Everybody's talking about it. You don't know?

James was compelled to do a Google search of the news in Witherton just to look less uninformed in front of Julie.

No. What was it? he asked instead.

You know that lawyer who was defending that one pedophile? Well, he attacked a woman yesterday and chewed her face, Julie's message said.

James reread that message three more times with a frown. He was half-convinced that Julie was just trying to play a prank on him, so this time, he actually went to his phone's browser and looked up Witherton's news.

Sure enough, Mark Sunderland, the lawyer who gained notoriety after publicly defending a pedophile, had gone crazy last night and assaulted a woman. James skimmed through the article, managing to catch that he had literally bitten off chunks of the victim's face before getting arrested. The police suspected that drugs were involved.

Damn. I'm not sure if I should be surprised or not, James wrote to Julie.

It seems to be happening a lot lately. Someone loses their mind and does something like this.

I'll accompany you to the beach if you're afraid of going alone, James wrote with a smiley face that was winking. His throat went dry as he waited for Julie's reply to the flirtatious remark.

I would love that! Her message came through moments later. **Maybe we could go this weekend?**

James resisted the urge to reply with "it's a date." **Deal,** he simply said.

I should probably get back to work. This sports article isn't going to write itself, Julie said with a smiley face plastered at the end of the message.

Don't work too hard, James wrote before shoving the phone into his pocket.

He picked up his keys and wallet and exited the house.

***

He also needed to buy cigarettes, he realized while driving his Honda toward the city. Police and ambulance sirens blared a lot more frequently today. Hearing sirens in Witherton was a normal daily occurrence. Hearing them in the quantities that they occurred today made them impossible to ignore.

James drove past a cop car with flashing blue and red lights that was parked on the side of the street. He managed to catch a glimpse of two police officers restraining a woman who was thrashing and screaming her lungs out.

I hear you, lady. I hate living here just as much as you do, James thought to himself.

He parked the car in front of Kroger and stepped outside. He ignored the voices of people arguing somewhere in the distance as he entered the store.

James pulled out a cart, suddenly realizing that he had no idea what he needed to buy for lunch. What did he want to make, anyway? It had been a while since he cooked anything at all, so he decided that chicken and some potatoes would probably be challenging enough for him.

A security guard bumped into his cart as he rushed past James and disappeared behind one of the aisles.

"No apology needed," James mumbled to himself since the guard was already long gone.

He rolled his cart through the aisle containing chips, looking for adequate snacks for later when he watched movies. A crash sounded from the far end of the store, snapping James's head in the direction of the sound. Echoing distorted the shouts that ensued, making the words indiscernible. A man was yelling, and then a female voice responded in an equally loud manner.

James couldn't see what was going on from here, but he decided that the best course of action would be to steer clear of the aisle. When he reached the deli section, the worker on the other side was fixated on the TV above.

"…reported that the woman sustained heavy injuries by the time the police intervened. The motive of the assault remains unclear as of the time of the report," the man on the news said as the camera panned to two police officers escorting a handcuffed man who was kicking and screaming, his head twitching.

"Hey," James tried to grab the attention of the deli worker.

The man's eyes remained glued to the screen a moment longer before finally averting to James.

"What can I get for you?" the man asked.

"Two pounds of chicken breast, please," James said.

The deli worker hastily put a piece of paper on top of the scale then slapped some wet chicken on top of it. The scale showed a little more than two pounds. James gave the worker a nod of approval, but the worker was already packaging the meat.

"Here you go," he said as he slapped the price sticker on it and handed it to James across the counter.

His eyes were already back watching the news on the TV even before James took the meat. By the time everything James needed was in his cart, another crash came from the store, this one much louder than the one before, riddled with an explosion of glasses breaking. Then came a shrill scream that made James stop dead in his tracks and jerk his head in the direction of the sound.

This is exactly why I rarely leave the house, James thought to himself as he approached the cashier.

While the items were being scanned, James's phone vibrated in his pocket again. He took it out, hoping for a message from Julie. The little exclamation mark next to the EMERGENCY ALERTS caught his attention. James had only once received an emergency message, and it had been just a test message. Something about receiving the message now made him feel restless. He tapped on the message to see what it was about.

Public Safety Alert
All citizens are advised to return to their homes immediately. Please remain indoors with doors securely locked. For emergency help, dial 911. Further instructions to be expected.

When James looked up, the cashier was also staring at his own phone; at the same message, no doubt. Worry crossed the cashier's face as he stared at the screen, the glow of the phone reflected in his glasses. He hurriedly scanned the rest of the items and waited for James to pay him.

A group of people walked into the store just as James exited. They were moving with hurried steps, their heads frantically jerking left and right, their eyes wide as they exchanged incoherent words among each other. Scoffing, James packed his groceries in his car and smoked one Marlboro before driving off toward home.

KRISTA

The air was ripe with an urgency that flowed through the entire waiting room. Hospital staff buzzed in and out with hurried steps while shouting to their coworkers. Patients sat, some with their heads down, some jerking upright whenever a nurse or a doctor walked by as if hoping that their presence would end their waiting.

Voices permeated the air: panicked speaking of new visitors at the reception desk, worried whispering among the patients, and occasionally, a dissatisfied voice arguing with a staff member about the long waiting times.

There were other noises, too, those that seemed so normal in a hospital that they were no more bothersome than a howl of the wind—sneezing, sniffling, and most frequently, persistent coughing that seemed to always come from one end or another like communication being bounced back and forth.

Krista held Nelson close with one arm around him, the tense atmosphere worrying her. She nervously glanced up from time to time to see if Eric was coming back. He had left minutes prior to check whether they would have their appointment for Nelson soon.

It was supposed to be thirty minutes ago, but their doctor was still nowhere in sight. That, coupled with the fact that the waiting room was so full that many patients had to stand, worried Krista.

"Mom, I don't feel good," Nelson said.

His head was slumping forward, his eyes fluttering. He'd been running a fever since that morning.

"Just a little longer, Nelson. The doctor will see us soon." Krista lied.

"Can we go home?"

"No, honey. Not until the doctor sees you."

Nelson let out a feeble groan at that. Krista ran a hand through his hair and found it was matted with sweat. He was getting worse. They needed to see the doctor fast. Once they did, everything would be all right. The doctor would tell them what to do to make Nelson better.

Krista looked up to search for Eric again. It took her a while to locate him because of the crowd, but she eventually found him standing in front of the reception desk, arguing with a nurse who was half-turned away from him, ready to leave.

Eric was giving her an angry look, but she didn't seem scared in the slightest. The intimidating appearance Eric had tried achieving by keeping his head shaved and his beard long didn't work. One good look at him was enough to see what a gentle face he had.

The nurse told him something, shook her head— always a bad sign—and then left, leaving Eric with his famous "I'm gonna kill somebody" look.

He strode past the crowded waiting room back toward his wife and child, and Krista didn't even need to ask him to know the news was bad.

"They're overwhelmed," Eric said.

Krista hoped it didn't mean what she thought it meant.

"Okay. Did they say how long we need to wait?" she asked.

"They say they can't see us right now."

"What?"

"The nurse said it's best to head home and try to keep Nelson's fever down."

"You've gotta be kidding me. Have you told her how bad Nelson is?"

"I did. She refused to budge. They say they have more urgent patients to tend to." Eric shrugged.

His seemingly blasé attitude made Krista angry. It made her want to go back to the nurse and explain why

Nelson needed to see a doctor right away as if Eric had said something wrong or missed an important piece of information.

Just then, a male doctor walked down the hallway. Before he could leave, Krista jumped on her feet. "Excuse me."

He showed no signs of noticing her, even though her hand was up and they were in a narrow hallway.

"Excuse me," she said again louder as she blocked his path.

The doctor stopped, the rigid look on his face making it more than obvious he didn't appreciate being stopped. Krista was not a confrontational person, except when it came to her son.

"We've been waiting here for hours. And now the nurse tells us to go home? Can you please check how long we need to wait? My son needs immediate medical help," she said.

"I'm sorry, ma'am. Lots of people here are in need of urgent care," the doctor said. "If the nurse told you to go home, then that's the best thing to do right now."

"Well, wait—"

"Doctor, you're needed here," someone said from one of the rooms.

"Excuse me." The doctor sidled past Krista before she could think of something to say.

"Honey, come on. Let's go home. We'll take care of Nelson." Eric's firm hand fell on Krista's shoulder.

She wanted to bat it away in anger. She didn't. Like most of the time she got angry, she subdued her rage.

"Fine," she said. "Nelson. Come on, baby. Let's go."

"I've got him. C'mere, champ." Eric took Nelson into his arms.

Nelson remained limp as his dad carried him across the waiting room. The waiting room was so crowded that it felt like being in a nightclub. Krista and Eric had to ask people to move so they could get through.

The closer they got to the exit, the more dense the crowd had become. Most heads were staring outside at something.

"Sorry. Just passing through," Eric said for what felt like a millionth time in the last minute while pushing through the crowd.

This time, no one moved. Their gazes remained fixed on whatever was out there while worried murmurs filled the air.

What was going on out there?

Just then, something loudly crashed behind them in the waiting room. Heads snapped. Screams filled the waiting room. The crowd started jostling in random directions.

At first, Krista couldn't see anything because of the people blocking her view, but as they ran around her, she caught glimpses of the commotion in the waiting room like snippets of a slide show.

A doctor was on the ground, and a man was on top of him. The man was attacking the doctor. Krista had been convinced that the attack was simply an angry patient who was told to go home like Krista and Eric.

Until she saw the blood.

Whose it was, she couldn't tell, nor where it had come from, but she was glad that the panicked people around her blocked her view after that.

The sense of politeness that Withertonians were so known for was gone. People bumped into her, sending her crashing into the person on the other side. Had no one been there to bump into, she would have fallen to the ground, and then her tiny frame would have been stomped.

"Nelson!" she shouted but could hardly hear her own voice over the shrieks in the waiting room.

Her sense of self-preservation was inactive, all energy fueling her feverish need to protect her son. It must have been the maternal instinct that she kept hearing about all her life.

She'd heard all sorts of heroic tales of mothers rushing into burning homes, lifting one-hundred-pound manholes, fighting off a pack of wild dogs, all for one purpose that drove them even to the brink of their own deaths—to protect their children.

Krista looked around, but she lost sight of her husband and son. Panic bloomed in her chest, threatening to squeeze her like a lemon.

She spun around, shouting Eric and Nelson's names, but they were nowhere in sight. She should have been able to spot Eric's bald head in the crowd easily.

Then, a hand closed firmly around her wrist. Before she could discover who it was, she was being pulled through the crowd. She glanced up at the person leading her, and assurance enveloped her when her eyes fell on the glistening, hairless top in front of her.

Just before they reached the exit, someone bumped hard into Krista, sending her stumbling toward her husband's back. She turned around and accidentally got a look at the back of the waiting room. She wished she hadn't done that.

Before she knew it, she was outside, and suddenly, the crowd no longer pressed up against her from all sides.

"Oh God!" Eric shouted as he broke into a run, pulling Krista along with him.

He was looking somewhere right, and Krista knew it was something bad, which was precisely why she refused to look. She didn't want to make the same mistake as in the waiting room.

But the peripheral vision caught way more than Krista thought possible. Even when that violent scene was out of her sight, Krista could still hear the moaning against the terrified screams.

She felt dazed as Eric dragged her to the car, and still, her thoughts focused on one and only one goal: keeping Nelson safe from all of it. Even when all three of them were safely inside the locked car, Krista kept all her energy focused on Nelson.

"Baby, are you okay? Are you hurt?" Krista asked.

Nelson was in the back seat, limp with fever, unaware of what was happening. Eric turned the key in the ignition. The engine whirred to life just as someone ran past their car, flailing their arms above their head as if they were on fire.

Eric stepped on the gas pedal, and the car lurched forward.

"Watch out!" Krista pointed at an oncoming Volvo.

Eric jerked the steering wheel to the right. The car swerved, missing the Volvo by mere inches. He got them out of the parking lot, and from there, the commotion was behind them.

"Jesus Christ!" Eric exclaimed.

Krista looked back at Nelson once more to make sure he wasn't hurt. Shame came over her for neglecting her husband's safety.

"Are you hurt?" she asked him.

"I'm fine," he said. "Just glad we're out of there."

With the danger subsiding, Krista's protective instinct waned, which made way for the images she refused to see while at the clinic.

The doctor who had been attacked in the waiting room stared blankly at the ceiling while rivulets of blood spurted out of his throat. The group of people in the parking lot hunched over a moaning person, pulling out her intestines and playing with them like a bunch of toddlers in the mud.

Relief and sickness enveloped Krista at the same time. It could have been her family on the ground like that with open throats and pulled entrails.

What if they had waited just a minute longer?

What if they found themselves in the spot of the doctor?

What if they crashed into the Volvo that didn't move out of the way even as it sped toward them?

The emotions that bubbled inside Krista were too potent. She buried her face in her hands and started sobbing in terror and relief.

Boris Bacic

DANIEL

"Is the front gate secure?!" Security Chief Skinner asked, his voice peppered with impatience and, Daniel noticed, fear.

Just five minutes ago, four security guards left to go outside. After a series of gunshots and screams, only two of them returned to the interior of the facility.

For as long as Daniel had worked at the lab, he'd always known Chief Skinner to be a person whose attitude never surpassed that of cavalier. His relaxed shoulders, hand loosely resting on the duty belt, and confident stride as he went on his daily patrol around the lab had become something of a trademark of the working place.

Now, his brow glistened with sweat, his eyes bulged, and the once-droopy shoulders stood so tense that the fabric of his uniform looked like it was ready to snap under his tight muscles. He got too close to the rookie security guard still in his early twenties standing in front of him.

"Speak up! Is it secure or not?!" the chief repeated.

Muffled screams outside oscillated in volume, keeping the entire team of surviving staff members on their toes. Peering at the glass walls, Daniel expected to see the crazies ramming the glass with their full body weights and bouncing off due to the thick pane that separated them from the interior. Blood would smear the pristine windows, and if the crazies combined their efforts, it wouldn't take long to break it down, no matter how sturdy it was.

The young security officer in front of Skinner bit his lip then gestured at something behind him, his eyes wide, as fragments of words came out of his mouth. "We, uh… the gate is… there's too many of th—"

"Goddammit!" the chief interrupted before motioning for the other guard standing behind him. Those three were the only security officers still alive. "Baker, with me."

He broke into a gait toward the front door, his hand no longer resting languidly on the gun but white-knuckling it with an intent to protect the premises.

With an intent to stay alive, Daniel thought to himself because this was no longer about anyone's moral obligations to protect the innocent or duties to the company that paid them their salaries. It was about survival.

Everything the group decided to do from that moment onward would have critical implications for their safety. Daniel hoped Chief Skinner's prior military experience would be enough to protect the unarmed personnel and help keep a cool head.

The chief pressed his palm against the door then turned toward the rookie and said, "You too, Elkins."

Daniel heard a gasp next to him. He ignored his coworkers as he focused on the crisis at hand. Currently, that crisis was whether the crazies would break into the facility and slaughter them like they did the passersby just outside the facility premises an hour earlier.

"Come on. Move it, people!" the chief said as he opened the door.

Baker followed the chief without an ounce of hesitation. The same could not be said of Elkins. His steps were small and timid, the hand on the gun reluctant, as if he couldn't decide whether drawing the firearm was a good idea or not.

Skinner held the door open for his security personnel as he drew the gun, his head swiveling left and right as he surveyed the area. Once the two guards were out, Skinner's gaze met with Daniel's, and he said, "Doc, listen up." Daniel's spine went erect with attention. "If we're not back soon, lock the whole place down. Don't open it for anyone."

Daniel ran up to the chief, not liking the responsibility bestowed on him. "You want me to lock you out? You can't possibly ask that of me."

"Doc, I need you to trust me like I'm trusting you, okay? If I can't keep you and your coworkers alive, then you'll have to do it." His voice was calm again but on the verge of cracking, running low on patience.

I was wrong. It isn't about survival. Skinner really believes in fighting to save the lives of other people.

If only he knew what kind of lives he was saving, though. Daniel forced himself to nod, determined to honor the chief's wish. He hated having such an enormous responsibility that possibly involved people's lives, but with all the higher-ups dead and only a few sections of the lab safe from the crazies, that difficult decision fell on Daniel's shoulders.

If he wanted to save lives, he might need to sacrifice lives. It was only a matter of doing the math to decide which number was bigger. Simple as that.

Chief Skinner seemed satisfied with Daniel's meager nod because he closed the door behind him and led his security team with hurried steps toward the gate. Daniel watched them until they were out of sight. He knew he would hear gunshots pretty soon, and he already dreaded them.

"Daniel?" Melissa asked as Daniel walked back to the group.

Her face was surprisingly blasé, considering the chaos surrounding them. She always struck Daniel as timid as a mouse, scared of even the slightest inconvenience. For all he knew, she *was* scared right then but was doing a good job hiding it.

Not like Richard Layton. The tall man in the lab coat who stood next to Melissa had turned pale despite his dark tan, the crags on his face accentuated by the overhead lights and the worry that he couldn't hide.

Doctor Edward Sharpe, the oldest of them all, conveyed calmness and panic at the same time. His face retained that focused stare that he always had in the lab when testing samples or looking at something under a microscope, but his body language communicated something entirely different.

The way he rubbed his thumb and forefinger against each other in a frantic manner, the way he skipped from one foot to the other, the way his head flitted in every direction as if he expected the crazies to get the drop on him out of nowhere all showed how utterly terrified he was.

Only four members of the science team remained. Daniel, Melissa, Sharpe, and Richard. If the guards didn't return soon, that number would remain the same. The clock was already ticking painfully; each passing second seemed to last an eternity, decreasing Daniel's belief that the guards would come back in one piece.

"What do we do now?" Richard asked.

"We should barricade all the other entry points," Daniel suggested, his eyes bouncing from furniture to furniture splayed around the ostentatious reception.

The company spared no expenses making a good first impression on visitors with their Omnia leather sofas, decorative plant pots, the now-inactive fountain statue, and abstractly shaped, spiral pieces of art that Daniel couldn't even name.

It took the group some time to move from the spots they were entrenched in. When Daniel grabbed the sofa and started dragging it toward the hallway door, the others broke out of their trances and began helping.

The scraping of furniture against the floor was obnoxiously loud, so much that Daniel kept glancing at the entrance, hoping not to see any movement—or to see it but discover it belonged to the security guards.

How long had it been since they left? Two minutes? Five? Couldn't have been more than that. The thin wisps of dread that had coiled around Daniel's limbs earlier blossomed into thorn-overgrown vines. If Skinner and the others didn't return soon, he'd need to lock the door, which would mean dooming the security guards.

Maybe they're already doomed.

"Daniel," Melissa had been calling to him for the past ten seconds, and he only just then registered it.

"What?" he asked, unable to stave off the hint of frustration that bubbled inside of him.

"Are we safe in here?"

"No, of course we're not fucking safe," he said, allowing the anger to take hold of him. No need to be ethically and politically correct toward his coworkers.

Not that ethics were ever involved in this goddamn company. Maybe just as a mask.

Discomfort washed over Melissa's face as she crossed her arms. Daniel was aware that he'd offended her, but it felt good to lash out in that moment. He had no intention of apologizing. Hurt feelings were not a priority.

"Are the guards okay?" Melissa asked.

"Do I look like a fucking psychic to you?"

Another satisfying twitch of her cheek muscle.

"So, what do we do then?" Richard upturned his palms.

"We wait for the crazies to break in and bash our brains in."

That only seemed to make Melissa even more uncomfortable but, in turn, caused a grin to tug at

Daniel's lips. Everyone had a coping mechanism for stressful situations. Daniel's was cracking unsavory jokes and feasting on the reactions of the people around him.

"You don't have to be a dick," Richard said, a response that surprised Daniel because, not only did he never swear, but he also always avoided arguments with his coworkers. It went to the point of agreeing to ideas he didn't believe would work just to avoid a conflict.

"We all need to keep our heads here," Doctor Sharpe said, the first smart response that came out of his mouth ever since this whole mess started.

Seeing Richard and Melissa shift expectantly in Sharpe's direction, Daniel realized he'd been too flippant, and it was costing him his credibility as the small group's leader.

"Fine. Let's find something we can use to defend ourselves," Daniel said.

"And then?" Richard asked.

"We wait for the guards. Then we'll go to the security room and assess the situation."

Gunshots echoed outside, too close to the facility. All research team heads turned instinctively toward the door, but no one was there. The growls outside grew louder.

"Find something to use, now. I'm going to lock the door," Daniel said.

He waltzed up to the door and input the passcode on the digit panel. His forefinger hovered above the OK button for a moment. His eyes flitted in the direction he'd seen the guards disappear, hoping he'd see them running back before it was too late.

More gunshots, and then a blood-curdling scream pierced the air. That was it. Daniel pressed the OK button. The door beeped and clicked to indicate it was locked. Had it been long enough for him to justify locking the door?

He stepped away and turned around to see Richard with a broom in his hands. What an idiot. He'd like to see him fight off even one crazy with such a useless tool. Melissa and Sharpe were still rummaging behind the desk, looking for a weapon.

"Okay," Daniel said. "Let's head up to security and—"

A thump behind him caused him to snap toward the sound. A figure was twisting the knob, unable to open it. It was the chief security guard. When he realized the door wouldn't open, he looked up at Daniel and banged on the door.

"You gotta let him in!" Melissa shouted.

"I know!" Daniel rushed to the door and frantically input the passcode, digit after digit.

"Open up! Open it!" Chief Skinner demanded, his head jerking intermittently from the door to the spot where he and the other guards had gone just minutes ago.

Where were the other two guards? Daniel assumed he already had the answer to that question.

"Hurry!" Richard shouted.

Daniel pressed OK. The display lit up with a red ERROR message. In his hurry, he must have input the wrong number.

"Fuck!" he shouted as he began inputting the code again.

"Come on, damn you!" Skinner pounded on the door. It was so sturdy that his hits came as dull and muffled thuds.

"What are you doing?! Let him in!" Melissa shrieked.

"I'm trying!"

A dashing figure caught Daniel's periphery. A man covered in blood from head to toe was sprinting directly at Skinner, hands outstretched forward, jaw unhinged as he screamed.

Daniel finished the code sequence and pressed OK again. ERROR.

"Come on!" Melissa shouted.

The guard raised his pistol and fired a single bullet. The crazy man's head kicked back, and he slid headlong across the ground, ceasing all movement. Daniel pressed each number slowly this time to make sure he got it right.

More crazies came into view. Skinner fired bullet after bullet, taking them down with finesse. He went for headshots, but he shot one of the crazies—a young woman—in the throat. That staggered but didn't stop the woman from advancing despite the blood that gushed out of her throat.

She threw herself on Skinner just as he fired a stray bullet. They were on the ground, wrestling, more crazies quickly approaching. How fucking many of them were there?!

"Dan!" Melissa shouted.

Daniel had finished the code but was refusing to press the OK button. It was risky. What if he accidentally let the crazies inside?

Skinner bucked his hips and got the crazy woman off him. Blood smeared the concrete floor as she writhed to get up. Dark red coated the front of Skinner's uniform, too.

The woman had lost momentum, probably due to the profuse bleeding. But she still wasn't giving up. She scrambled up to her feet just as Skinner punched her square in the face, sending her back down. He used that moment to turn around and shoot the incoming crazies.

Skinner was tougher than he looked. Even if Dan didn't open the door, he'd survive. Skinner would survive because people like him were trained for only two things: killing and surviving.

That was exactly why they needed Skinner inside the building with them. If anyone was going to keep them safe, it was him.

Fuck!

Daniel slammed the OK button, more on a whim than in a calculated decision. The door beeped, and the lock clicked. That click was louder than a thousand gunshots because, the moment it happened, Skinner's eyes weren't the only ones glued to the door.

Daniel could visually see the consequences of that single, simple decision unfolding in front of him like a video played at fast-forward speed. Like a computer that had shut down before he could properly save the file he was working on, there was nothing he could do.

The noise of the click had drawn the attention of the crazies, and they broke from the security guard toward the entrance, their snarls foreshadowing what they were about to do.

Boris Bacic

BEN

Ben sat at the edge of the bed, scrolling through social media on his phone. A text message from Melissa popped up at the top of the screen.

Something crazy is going on in the city. Think you can pick me up from work?

Ben swiped the message away, refusing to be bothered to ask her what she meant nor to reassure her that everything would be all right. He'd call her later when he got the chance. Or they would talk when she finished work.

Ben had a specific routine he loved to follow during the day, and he hated when Melissa disrupted that routine with her sudden whims. If he went to pick her up from work, he would need to move his training session to an hour later, and that was when the gym would become too crowded.

The mattress behind Ben shifted. Nails gently raked his back.

"You have that look on your face. Is it your wife?" Stephanie asked.

Ben turned his head toward her. She was lying on her side, one hand under her head, her hair splayed on the mattress, her nude breasts exposed, belly flat.

She looked so much more divine in bed than Melissa, he had to notice. He tried not to compare them, but it was impossible.

"Yeah," he simply said.

Stephanie's gaze bore into Ben. He hated that gaze because it felt as though she was trying to read his soul. Also because it reminded him of the way Melissa used to look at him in the early days of their marriage.

"What does she want?" Stephanie asked.

"For me to pick her up from work." Ben's reply was curt.

"Right now?"

"Yeah."

"Can't you stay five more minutes?"

"No. It sounds like this is urgent."

"I see. Okay. I'll get dressed, then." Defeat colored her voice.

Stephanie stopped caressing Ben's back. He knew she was bothered by the fact that the attention that was supposed to be given to her was divided with Melissa. Nothing he could do about that. Stephanie knew what she was getting into when she first started flirting with Ben. She'd seen the ring on his finger. She just couldn't resist getting a bite out of the forbidden fruit.

What was it with women being into taken guys, anyway? He could conveniently forget his wedding ring at home, and the girls he flirted with would treat him like he was a bum begging for drug money. But the moment the magic ring was on, it was as if it cast a spell on the women that spoke to him.

Stephanie and Ben had established a list of rules for their affair when they first started dating, but he could sense that she was growing more discontent with that sort of relationship.

He saw it in the way she jealously glanced at his phone whenever it buzzed with a notification or when she asked him to stay just a minute longer, or when she kept asking him how things were between him and Melissa; as if she was hoping for their marriage to deteriorate.

It wouldn't be long before she asked him if he planned on divorcing his wife, and that would probably be the end of their affair. Ben had made it very clear at the start of the affair that Melissa would always come first, but

Stephanie seemed to forget that more and more often lately.

It was only natural it would come to that. She was only nineteen, and nobody wanted to spend years of their life in a relationship as a spare. Ben liked having Stephanie around, and he liked having Melissa there, too. But if he had to choose, he'd always choose Melissa because she was one of a kind.

Stephanie, on the other hand, could easily be replaced by a pretty girl with a high libido.

Ben stood and got dressed. The air in the room became heavier, almost viscous. It wasn't the heated, stuffy kind of air after intense love-making. This was riddled with tension. Ben didn't need to look hard to locate the source that emanated it. It was right there, on the other side of the bed, putting on a bra.

The right thing to do would have been to say something, perhaps ask Stephanie what was wrong. But if he did that, it would open the door for her to tell him exactly what was wrong, and he didn't want to deal with it today. Maybe next time.

"Uber seems unavailable," Ben said with a frown after trying to request a ride online.

He tried Lyft but got the same results. That strange. He tried calling a cab service, but the line was dead.

"What the hell. This is weird," he said.

"What is it?" Stephanie asked.

She had gotten dressed and was pulling her hair into a ponytail. Ben often told her he didn't like her wearing her hair like that. He said it was because it reminded him too much of his ex, but the truth was that Stephanie's forehead was too big for a ponytail.

"I can't seem to reach anyone for a ride home," he said.

"I'll give you a ride," she said. "I need to head downtown to take care of something anyway."

To take care of something.

It was as if she was deliberately being vague. She probably was, hoping to see if Ben would bite, become jealous. It was working, but he wouldn't let her know about that. The moment she thought she had even an ounce of control over him was when she would start exerting that power to make demands. Ben would not fall for that age-old trick.

"Sure. That would be great."

"I just need to run an errand while there. You wouldn't mind waiting a bit while I do it, would you?"

There it was again, the second hook thrown into the water. Ben almost grinned at the cat-and-mouse game he and Stephanie were playing. She was still green, though, not nearly as experienced as Ben. He knew every trick in the book so he wouldn't be swayed by it.

"Yeah, no problem." He grinned.

"Great. Let me just get my things," she said as she left the room.

"I'm gonna need a minute to put on some makeup!" she shouted from the bathroom. "You can watch some TV in the meantime if you want!"

Oh, she was fishing so badly.

"Sure thing!" he shouted back with a grin.

That expression quickly downturned into a scowl because he realized Stephanie's bait was working, and he was dying to know what that "errand" was and whether it even existed.

To occupy himself while waiting for her, he scrolled Facebook. Every now and again, Witherton news would pop up, either from his friends' feeds or from suggested pages like *Witherton Triumphs*.

He couldn't ignore the news that some kind of an attack was happening on Candlewood Boulevard. A picture of police and ambulance vehicles parked in front of body bags caught his attention.

The article was vague, so it was impossible to tell if this was a terrorist attack or the work of an individual, or something entirely different. The comments provided no answers, save for the typical speculations customary for every social media post.

"Hey, do you know what's going on on Candlewood Boulevard?" he asked Stephanie.

"What was that?" she shouted back from the bathroom.

"Do you have any idea what's happening on Candlewood Boulevard?" he repeated.

"No, what? Do they have some kind of festival there again?"

"What? No. Some kind of an attack. Multiple people injured."

"Oh?" Stephanie sounded blasé about the whole thing.

Her reaction was weird because this was Witherton, and Witherton rarely had tragedies of such proportions.

"Well, anyway, avoid Candlewood Boulevard because of the traffic, maybe try Main Street. Should be less crowded," Ben said.

"Okay. Sounds good," Stephanie said. "Ready to go?"

When she stepped out of the bathroom, she looked the way she did before their date. The post-sex disheveled hair and ruined makeup were gone. It was as if Stephanie had stepped in and another person had stepped out.

In fact, she looked like she was getting ready for another date. Ben dismissed that thought—and the pang of jealousy—from his mind.

"Yeah, let's go." He stood.

Stephanie grabbed her keys and strolled out of the apartment, a little too perky for someone going downtown for an errand. Once again, Ben found himself on the verge of asking where exactly she was going but resisted that urge. He didn't want to let her have the upper hand.

Still, it was a difficult pill to swallow. Yes, Stephanie was free to date whoever she wanted, but he didn't like that. He liked having her as his property alone.

The moment they stepped out into the street, the air somehow felt different. *Dead but at the same time hectic* was the description that came to Ben's mind, and he couldn't define why. Something was different then than it had been an hour ago when Stephanie picked him up in front of Burger King.

It was as if the city had gone quiet, but the blaring sirens in the distance were there to remind him that Witherton was still very much alive. Tires screeched in the distance until Ben realized those weren't tires at all. It was a scream.

He looked toward Stephanie to see if he was imagining things. She seemed oblivious to the whole thing as she strode to her car and unlocked it, waiting for Ben to step inside. She was still shining. In fact, she looked like she couldn't wait to get rid of Ben.

The jealousy that had pricked his mind made way for the news of the massacre on Candlewood Boulevard. Something big was going on, and Ben knew it wouldn't be good.

PIERCE

"We're almost at the LZ!" the chopper pilot shouted.

Pierce didn't like not knowing what the unit was heading into. It wasn't an uncommon occurrence, but he still disliked it nonetheless. Secrecy meant something that wasn't supposed to get out had leaked, and it was the team's job to clean it up.

The other team members apparently shared his sentiment because Shepherd leaned forward and asked, "Captain, do we know anything about the mission?" She adjusted her belt as she spoke.

"Just what we've been briefed on," Captain Reynolds said. "We'll get more intel once we land."

Shepherd leaned against the wall of the chopper, her nose wrinkled at the unsatisfactory response from Reynolds.

"Pierce, you're originally from Witherton, right?" Murphy asked. His round cheeks were squeezed by the straps of the helmet.

"Yeah." Pierce nodded. "But I moved out of there when I was sixteen."

"That's an early age to go."

Pierce shrugged.

He could have talked about how he ran away from home after shooting his alcoholic stepdad one night for beating the shit out of him every day. This was not the time for that story, though.

To his teammates, it would be something to help pass the time. To Pierce, it would be a distraction. The idea of returning to his hometown already bothered him enough. Recalling memories from the worst part of his life wouldn't help him in any way.

His hands were clammy under his gloves, and he could hardly focus on the conversation between his teammates in the chopper.

Witherton. Why the fuck did it have to be Witherton?

And yet, as he stared at the rifle between his legs propped up against the floor on its stock, he knew he wasn't the same person he'd been that day when he ran. The moment he pulled that trigger and shattered his stepdad's kneecap, he became a different person—a caterpillar coming out of its cocoon as a butterfly.

"I heard it's cleanup," Lincoln said, causing heads to turn toward him. He shrugged. "What? Why else would they send our unit on a mission so abruptly, right after the outbreak, on a need-to-know basis?"

"Don't jump to conclusions, Lincoln," the captain said. "We don't know what we're supposed to do yet."

"Whatever it is, they're sending us *inside* the city. That's bad enough," Murphy said. "We're going on a suicide mission."

"Hope y'all wrote your wills." Lincoln quipped.

"That's enough," Captain Reynolds said. "We're not here to speculate. Now, get your asses up. We're almost there."

Shepherd cast a glance out the window, started to turn back, then jerked her head back at what caught her attention outside.

"Holy fuck," she said. "Look at this shit."

"What?" Lincoln asked as he spun to peek out, and his brow furrowed.

Murphy stood up and walked over to the window that Shepherd was looking through and said, "Huh."

Their child-like reactions piqued Pierce's interest. He crossed over to see what the fuss was all about.

"Jesus," he muttered under his breath.

His teammates had been right, he noted.

Although the details about the outbreak itself weren't disclosed to the unit, it hadn't taken Pierce long to put two and two together. The suppression of news about Witherton was already an indicator that something messed up was at play.

The tall walls that enclosed the entire city, stretching as far as the chopper's altitude allowed them to see, only confirmed it.

"You getting homesick yet, Pierce?" Lincoln, ever the loudmouth asked.

"It's like I'm looking at a completely different place," Pierce said.

He'd never seen the city from this point of view, except in pictures, and those were always touched up to look nicer. The gray clusters of buildings that sprouted within the walls and curlicues of smoke rising around various spots of the enclosed city were a far cry from the idyllic picture represented on Witherton's postcards.

It was a mess. Although the city looked dead, Pierce didn't let that fool him. Witherton was very much brimming with life—like microorganisms invisible to the naked eye.

If his mother and stepfather hadn't died before the outbreak, they were sure to be dead now. His mother had never been the athletic type, and his stepdad would have a hard time making a run with what was left of that knee.

Pierce averted his gaze from the ruined city and focused on the exterior. APCs were parked outside. Soldiers buzzed from place to place while others stood guard on top of the walls, overlooking the city. Pierce imagined piles of corpses at the foot of the wall—infected and people alike who tried to claw their way out to freedom before getting gunned down.

Beyond the wall, a second line of defense was erected, barricades consisting of sandbags, not nearly as impressive as the walls themselves.

"How the fuck did they get those up so fast?" Murphy asked.

"They probably had them ready exactly for this kind of scenario," Shepherd replied. "Still, I can't imagine the work needed to put something like this together. Nothing comes out of that."

"And we're going inside. Nice." Lincoln grinned.

The chopper began its descent.

Pierce suddenly became aware of how tightly he was clutching his rifle. He forced himself to relax, remembering that they were only approaching a well-defended outer perimeter crawling with friendlies.

It wasn't the anticipation of setting foot inside a mission hot zone that caused perspiration to break out on his brow. Something else gnawed at Pierce, something he couldn't pinpoint—like a mosquito that stung him and then retreated, only to return as soon as he dropped his guard as if to remind him it was still there.

It was this place. It had to be.

It's just a town full of bad memories. It can't hurt me.

Pierce had believed he'd conquered his demons when he left Witherton and became a soldier. Gazing at the remnants of the place he once called home, he understood how wrong he was.

He hadn't defeated his demons. He'd only buried them deep enough to forget they ever existed. And they were finally finding their way out, the soil they'd been buried under too soft to keep them entombed.

"At least, we'll have someone with us who knows the town inside out. Right, Pierce?" Shepherd grinned her pearly grin at Pierce.

"If we walk past *Joe's Meat*, we can stop for a break. They got the best burgers," Pierce joked.

"Fuck burgers. I wanna see where Witherton's best place for drinking is," Lincoln said.

Looking at his teammates, one thing dawned on Pierce.

He'd have no choice but to forget about his demons the moment they set foot inside Witherton. If he didn't, he'd not only be endangering himself but his entire team, too.

The helicopter touched ground, and the door opened.

"Move out." Reynolds jutted his head toward the exit.

Then they were out of the chopper, on solid ground, and Pierce was once again a soldier on a mission, and not a boy afraid of his past.

JAMES

Lunch wasn't restaurant-worthy, but it was good enough. It felt refreshing to eat something as simple as chicken breast and air-fried potatoes. James continued watching Ash vs Evil Dead on Netflix since he was in the mood for something that wouldn't require too much brain activity.

He glanced at his phone every now and again, the emergency alert constantly on his mind, distracting him from the gory scenes of Ash killing Deadites with his chainsaw hand. He was tempted to text Julie and ask her if she got the same message, but he remembered that she was working on an article, and he didn't want to bother her during work time.

Five episodes later, he paused the TV and went outside for some fresh air—and a healthy cigarette break. The sky went from sunny to overcast. That kind of weather always made James sleepy. He stood in his driveway, looking left and right down the empty street and exhaling plumes of smoke.

The garage of his neighbor across the street opened. Sean's sedan reversed out of the garage and onto the street with screeching tires. James's eyes fell on Sean in the driver's seat. His face was contorted into a grimace, his eyes wide, his hands white-knuckling the steering wheel.

The front door opened, and Sean's wife barged outside with a suitcase. She closed the door behind her, locked it, and clumsily loped to the car. James raised a hand to greet her. He thought her eyes fell briefly on him, but she gave no indication of seeing him before stepping inside the car.

Then, they drove off with another symphony of screaming tires against the road. James frowned and shook his head, weirded out by their behavior. He stubbed his cigarette on the rim of the trash can that he specifically put out for his smoke breaks (he didn't like smoking too much inside the house) and went back inside.

The moment he closed the door behind him was when he heard it.

A steady alarm was coming from the TV. His eyes immediately fell on the screen. It was no longer the paused, blurry screen that James had left it on. Instead, red bloomed on the screen with the message EMERGENCY BROADCAST occupying the middle of the screen.

Reality suddenly crashed over James like a piano dropped from the roof. He had ignored all those signs, but it was clear now that something was up. The people acting all crazy, the emergency alert that he had received, and now this?

His first thought was that Russia was nuking them. James strode over to the couch and plopped into it, his unblinking eyes focused on the screen. The steady beeping that was coming from the TV turned into an electric, crackling noise, similar to the one the old dial-up internet used to make when establishing a connection. The sound changed multiple times, probably to better catch the attention of whoever was in the room.

Silence replaced the noise. James swallowed and steadied his breathing, straining to catch every sound that came from the TV. It only just then occurred to him that he could turn up the volume. He grabbed the remote and held down the plus button until he could hear the buzzing of the screen. A deep, male voice boomed from the TV, startling James.

"This is an emergency government broadcast for the citizens of Witherton. Stay inside your homes. Lock your doors, cover your windows, and avoid making too much noise. Do not go outside under any circumstances. You will receive further instructions soon." After a short pause, the message started again. "This is an emergency broadcast for the citizens…"

James turned the volume down then, but not entirely, because he wanted to hear the further instructions that would be delivered. He leaned back on the couch, his hands resting on his knees, his brain processing the emergency message.

And then it hit him that he still hadn't locked his door.

He jumped to his feet and rushed to the front door. For some reason, he looked through the peephole. He could see his neighbor's open garage in a fisheye lens view, but other than that, the street was empty. James turned the lock twice and then draped the curtains over the windows. A sense of pride overcame him as he did so. His mother had told him that the curtains were gaudy, but he'd installed them because, at one point during the day, the sun fell directly on the living room area, which made it impossible to see the screen of the TV properly.

With the room veiled in darkness, James sauntered into the kitchen and locked the backdoor, too. He glanced into his backyard from the window in front of the sink. He didn't know what he expected to see, but standing in front of the pane of glass made him feel incredibly vulnerable, so he stepped away from it and returned to the living room.

The house looked unnatural devoid of light. The only illumination in the room came from the red screen of the TV. The message was still on a loop, the pre-recorded warning playing in the same, monotone voice.

James was restless. He felt like there was more he needed to do, but he couldn't tell what. He sat back on the couch and unlocked his phone. He had received another emergency alert, this one informing him of the same steps as the TV.

James tried to make sense of the warning.

Stay inside. That one was pretty self-explanatory. Inside was safer.

Lock your doors. That one was understandable as well. But the question was: Why would they need to lock the doors? What was the threat? A shooter on the loose? An escaped inmate? A terrorist attack? Maybe it was a natural disaster. No, that wasn't possible. Witherton never had any natural disasters, except that one minor flood that happened a year ago.

Cover your windows. That one baffled James the most. It meant that it wasn't a natural disaster in question. It was a threat in the form of a human. Perhaps a crazed gunner killing everyone indiscriminately in the area? James hadn't heard any gunshots.

The image of his neighbors driving off in a hurry flashed in his mind. They looked scared. The instructions specifically said to stay put, and they were doing the opposite. Did they get their news from a different source?

James lit a cigarette as he looked up Witherton news again. They were a lot more colorful this time. It was as if James had been asleep for years and woken up to an apocalyptic new world. Articles about people violently assaulting passersby covered every headline. The rumors followed closely behind.

It was something the government put in the water. It was a radio wave experiment by the CIA to alter the minds of individuals. It was the unforeseen side effects of vaccines. It was something in the air that evaporated and caused people to behave so crazy.

Already, groups were formed on Facebook to loudly express their distrust in the government. A message popped up on the screen.

Are you seeing this?? It was Julie.

The news? Yeah, it's crazy. How are things at your place? James replied.

It's insane. People are losing their minds. I just saw someone shoot another person and hijack their car.

James lived in the suburban area of Witherton while Julie was downtown, so it was expected that things would be wilder on her end. Still, to know that the peace-loving and polite people of Witherton would resort to such violence seemed out of this world.

Wait, really? James sent the message.

Yes! The guy just shot him and pulled him out of the car. I tried calling the police, but they weren't responding. James, I'm scared. What's going on?

For the first time since knowing her, James could sense Julie's fear. He wanted to tell her that everything would be okay. He wanted to believe in that himself. But if there was one thing that James hated, it was making promises that he couldn't uphold.

Where are you now? Are you safe? Do you want me to call you? He sent the texts one by one in rapid succession.

I'm inside my apartment. No, don't call me. I'm afraid they might hear me.

James's fingers went cold at that last sentence. He gulped against his dry throat, the need for another cigarette rising. He sat ramrod straight as his fingers hovered above the touchpad keyboard, wondering what to say to Julie.

Okay, stay hidden. Is your apartment secure?

He had to type that message in multiple times because he made typos along the way.

James, Julie's message came through. Then a long pause before her next message. **They're inside.**

The cold spread from James's fingers to his extremities. A frozen snake slithered down his neck and inside the back of his shirt. He stared at the last message, the sense of foreboding refusing to abate.

They're inside.

Who is? James typed. **Julie, just stay there, okay? Stay hidden, and don't make a sound.**

But Julie wasn't responding. Even when minutes went by and James sent another **Julie??** message to her, there was no response. He was on the verge of calling her, but he didn't want to put her in any danger. Calling the police crossed his mind, but he didn't know Julie's address. What would he even say? His friend whose address he didn't know was in danger?

James's foot tapped on the floor. The sound was too loud, even against the repeating TV message. He swiveled in the direction of the window, tempted to peek outside.

"Cover your windows," the man on the TV said, a sentence that James needed to hear in order to dissuade himself from doing anything stupid.

He folded his hands on top of his head, not liking the idea of sitting around while the government decided to take matters into its own hands. Every now and again, James checked his phone to see if Julie would respond.

He wanted to continue watching Ash vs Evil Dead to pass the time, but he didn't want to miss any instructions if they appeared on TV. At one point, after what felt like hours of sitting in front of the dimly lit room, his phone buzzed.

James practically jumped to read the message. It was from his internet provider informing him of better packages that he could purchase. James clenched his jaw, wondering how those assholes managed to reach him at a time like this.

He entered the conversation with Julie again, hoping to see new messages there. The last one was the one he'd sent: **Julie??** He didn't like looking at Julie's final message to him. **They're inside.** He forced himself to exit the chat and paced around the house.

His eyes kept flitting to the TV, hoping for further instructions to arrive. The longer he waited, the more restless he became. Why was the government being so vague about this? Something was going on; that much was sure.

It crossed James's mind that maybe it was a falsely sent alarm that caused widespread panic in the town. It wouldn't be the first time it happened. People were prone to becoming violent once their basic amenities were stripped from them. And in a place where so many people conceal-carried, it was only a matter of time before one disaster escalated into two, two into ten, and so on.

James's train of thought was interrupted by a sound. Something that sounded like a clipped cry.

And it came from outside his door.

HEATHER

Abby was occupied with the puzzle she was diligently trying to put together, so Heather didn't need to pay attention to her too much. Just a glance from time to time to make sure she wasn't doing anything troublesome.

Heather kept checking her phone for notifications from Tracy or Dwayne. When none came, she entered the chat with Tracy once more, only to realize her last message failed to send. She tapped "retry" and waited. It failed again.

She tried calling her, but the line dropped. She was partly relieved that she didn't need to talk to her, but it raised other concerns. Like what was going on? Why were the phones down? Should she try to call the cops?

Heather went on the internet. It still worked, for the most part, but she found that some of the websites were blocked. She turned on the TV to see what the news said. The first channel that filled the screen showed chaos in the street as a female journalist reported the situation.

"Please be quiet, Abby," Heather said as she listened to the news lady. She was highly irritable ever since she had the interaction with Dwayne.

"Police are having difficulty containing the situation. It is unknown what the cause of such behavior is, but it appears to be widespread in Witherton. The government -has sent a notification to all citizens to stay inside their homes and wait for further instructions."

"Red-eyed people." Abby pointed at the screen as a man with bloodshot eyes came into view.

He was running toward the camera and screaming, face contorted in such a grimace that veins bulged on his forehead and neck. Just when he reached the camera and it jerked upward, the footage cut out.

Other channels reported the same. It at least gave Heather solace to know that Baldwin wasn't the only affected neighborhood and that the emergency alert text she'd received was not a hoax. That meant that someone had to do something to help the citizens of Witherton sooner or later.

"Heather, when can we go outside?" Abby asked.

"Later, Abby, okay?"

"When?"

"I don't know."

"In a few hours?"

"Probably not."

"Why not?"

"Because I said so."

Abby looked down at the puzzle, fiddling with one piece. Heather bit the inside of her cheek. Lately, she snapped a lot at Abby and then immediately regretted it. Most of the time. Not always, though. Abby tested her nerves a lot. Sure, she didn't do it on purpose, but she still did it, and Heather could only take so much.

Heather didn't realize how much she valued time away from Abby until today. As much as she hated dealing with creepy customers at work, after two days off at home plus another because of the red-eyed people outbreak, she felt like she was already losing her mind.

Not to mention she usually got out of the apartment on her days off, at least, for an hour or two to buy groceries or take a walk. She hadn't done that since her last shift, so she'd practically spent seventy-two hours with Abby.

She couldn't even catch five minutes of solitude in the bathroom before Abby knocked to ask if she could come in.

Snapping was bound to happen, and Heather was sure it would only become worse in the upcoming days.

There was no news about a rescue plan or anything concrete, and being in the dark like that was what drove Heather insane. If she at least knew something was being done about the situation, she would have been at ease.

Then there was also the pressure of not knowing what would happen with her work once this whole thing blew over. She kept glancing at her phone, hoping for a ping or vibration, something to let her know everything was okay and her not showing up to work was excusable.

But when evening came and nothing changed, Heather sent Abby to bed while she stayed up, listening to the screams outside. She fell asleep close to dawn and was woken up by Abby, who was perky, rested, and demanding Heather's full attention.

Over the next three days, one by one, the channels on the TV went dark, until all that remained was the emergency broadcast telling citizens to stay inside. Soon, the internet went out, too. That was bad. Very bad.

"Fuck!" Heather yelled out of frustration on the evening of the third day.

It was past Abby's bedtime by then, and Abby was with her in the room.

"Sis said a bad word!" Abby put one hand over her mouth and pointed a finger at Heather.

"Go to your room, Abby."

Heather fiddled with the settings on her phone to see if she could fix the internet. A desperate attempt that she knew would have no results. She felt like crying. What was she supposed to do? Keep waiting? They only had enough food in the apartment for a couple of days. What if no one came after it ran out?

"Bad word! Bad word!" Abby chanted in a sing-song voice. "Can I say it, too? Sis, can I say the bad word? Sis?"

She was tugging the hem of Heather's shirt. Heather's already painful headache was growing with each shrill word Abby cried out.

"I told you to go to your room, Abby."

"Sis! I want to say the bad word! Can I say the—"

A crack filled the room. Silence took over. Abby stood in front of Heather, tears welling up in her eyes as she held a hand over her red cheek. Heather's palm still vibrated from how hard she'd slapped Abby. All of a sudden, regret and guilt took her over, making her want to cry even more.

"Abby... I'm so sorry. I didn't mean to. I..." she stammered, but Abby was already running into her room.

"Abby!" Heather called out, but Abby slammed the door shut in her face. Heather banged on the door. "Abby, open the door."

It was unlocked, but she didn't want to go in without Abby's permission because she could throw tantrums.

"I'm sorry, Sis. I didn't mean to. I don't know what got into me. I'm sorry. I swear I'll never do it again," she said.

"Go away!" Abby's muffled voice shouted from the room.

It was not the time to try and console Abby. Heather would give her space and try to talk to her later—or tomorrow. Muffled sobbing came from inside just as Heather stepped away from the door. The need to cry tightened in her chest, to let out all the pent-up emotions that had been eating away at her for so long.

She wiped the meager tears that blurred her vision, sniffled, and retreated into the living room, hating her parents for leaving her alone with Abby.

DANIEL

Daniel pressed his palms against the door, but it was futile.

The crazy that rammed his body into the door was a guy built like an NFL player.

Daniel flew backward, hitting the floor on his rear. He only vaguely registered that the door was now wide open.

More terrifyingly, the NFL crazy stood in front of him, and if he so much as wanted to rip Daniel's head out of his neck, he could do so with ease with those veiny, tree trunk-thick arms.

Not an NFL player. A bodybuilder, Daniel conjured the irrelevant thought as if he had nothing better to think about before death.

The reason why he was able to differentiate bodybuilding from NFL was because athletes used to come to Daniel all the time for hormone replacement therapies before he joined Welco Labs.

The man in front of him had muscles that were too proportional, too lean, not an ounce of fat under his skin. Behind that monstrous physique were countless days of meals prepped with surgical precision.

That and 800 mg of weekly testosterone injections.

The man's bloodshot eyes locked with Daniel's, ravenous and angry. Daniel knew he stood no chance against this truck of a man. His first instinct told him to curl into a ball and hope he didn't get crushed under the blows.

But before he could properly contemplate that, a hole exploded in the bodybuilder's Adam's apple with an ear-splitting bang, squirting a jet of blood that fell at Daniel's shoes. The man gurgled as he fell on his hands and knees, animalistic grunts escaping his throat as blood dripped from his neck to the floor in an ever-growing pool.

Behind him stood Skinner with his gun pointed at the man. He fired another shot, this time hitting the back of the man's head. The bodybuilder's eyes rolled in his head, and he fell into the pool of blood, no longer moving.

Years and years of discipline and hard work at the gym and rejected desserts in order to maintain the bodily aesthetics of a Greek god, and the only results the man would see from his dedication would be being a handsome corpse for a short time.

"Doc!" Skinner's voice snapped Daniel's attention up. The security guard was pushing his shoulder against the door, barely holding the horde of crazies off from opening it. "Lock it, now!"

The crazies pressed themselves against the door and the walls. It was just like Daniel had imagined it—blood smeared the glass, except he didn't account for the fact that there'd be mucus from the throat, bits of undigested food, and brown substance that—

Disgusting, Daniel thought to himself as he hopped to his feet and ran up to the pad on the wall.

He entered the code. This time, his fingers flew across all the right buttons without error. When he pressed OK, the lock clicked once more, securing the place. Skinner stepped away, pointing his gun at the crazies on the other side. They were pounding on the glass, but their efforts were futile.

For now.

Skinner lowered then holstered his gun. Only then did Daniel see him in full detail.

The top of his balding scalp was covered in blood, the beads of sweat that had coated his forehead trickling down to his neck. Splotches of red drenched the front of his uniform, which stank of something metallic.

Daniel felt the way Skinner looked. He hadn't realized it until then, but the close call that almost cost him—and everyone else—their lives left his heart strumming against his chest, cold sweat enveloping his back.

He was not cut out for this shit. He wasn't even supposed to be in this goddamn mess.

"Where are the others?" Melissa asked.

Skinner downturned his gaze then turned away from the crazies pressed against the glass. "We need to get out of here. Come on."

It was clear that Daniel was no longer the figure the others looked up to. Thank God. He could go back to worrying about his own survival. Skinner called the elevator and waited until the others were inside.

Daniel was still stuck in his spot, curiously gazing at the crazies.

They growled, hissed, screamed, and made inarticulate sounds as they scratched and bit at the glass in futility. Most of them were dirty, either from mud or blood. One woman suffered an open fracture of her forearm, and the bone that jutted out at the odd angle evidently didn't seem to bother her.

What happened to these people? They looked as if they'd lost a lot of their cognitive abilities, reducing them to animal-like, violent behavior.

It couldn't even be called predatory behavior because predators killed to eat their prey. These people didn't kill for food. They killed because... why exactly? Clearly, something drove them to such violent behavior—an instinct or an irresistible urge—but where had it come from? And why so suddenly?

"Doc?" Skinner called out. "We gotta move."

Daniel swiveled toward the group expectantly waiting at the elevator. His eyes fell on the dead bodybuilder on the ground.

"Doctor. Now," Skinner said, his inflection stern.

If Daniel didn't move soon, the security chief would throw him inside the elevator by force.

"I can't go yet," he said.

"Doctor." Skinner was on the verge of striding over to Daniel and hauling him to the elevator; Daniel could see it from the way his shoulders tensed and lips scrunched.

"I can't leave until I've secured this corpse and prepared it for an autopsy."

"What? There's no time for that bullshit. Come on, move your ass."

"Chief Skinner, this is very important. It could save lives. I need you to trust me like I trusted you when you went outside to secure the gate."

Skinner's nostrils flared with frustration. Daniel could tell the guard didn't like having his own words used against him.

"We'll come back for him, doc. Come on, just get into the elevator."

"No. We need to get him to the lab *now*."

Daniel could tell that Skinner wasn't the only one irritated with his insistence. His coworkers were restless in the elevator, waiting for him to get in so they could move, eager to put distance to the crazed people pressed up against the glass.

Skinner's face went slack, and Daniel knew then that the guard was going to cave, either because he could read how stubborn Daniel was or because he wanted to get things over with as soon as possible.

"Fine," Skinner said. "Let's get him inside the elevator."

He stamped to the bodybuilder and grabbed him by the back of the collar. With ease, he dragged the heavy man with one hand toward the elevator, leaving a fading trail of blood like a spent paintbrush.

The research members scooted to the corners of the elevator to make way for Skinner, their grimaces—especially Melissa's—showing how squeamish they were. Weird for a team of scientists to be so afraid of a corpse.

"Come on, doctor." Skinner gestured to the elevator.

Daniel nodded and stepped inside. He turned to face the crazies at the entrance before the elevator doors closed, and the elevator began ascending.

"I take it the other two guards are dead and the gate is lost?" Daniel asked.

He knew his voice sounded cold, but that wasn't his intention. He simply had no strength to strain it to match his inner turmoil.

Skinner said nothing, which was a confirmation to Daniel's question.

"What do you need the body for?" Richard asked.

"I like collecting them as trophies." Daniel's sarcasm evoked no laughter, which was expected, so he added, "To find out what's causing all of this."

"It's not just a few people," Melissa said. "I've seen the news. It's the entire town. I should be out there. My husband…"

"There's no way you can make it out there," Skinner said. "We're going to find help. The company has a helipad on the roof. All we gotta do is give them a call, and they'll come pick us up."

"Thank heavens." Melissa's face lit up with relief.

A similar reaction lit Richard's face. Daniel forced a smile through gritted teeth.

"How do you know they'll come?" Sharpe asked.

"That's how standard Welco evacuation works. It's in the contract. The company works with high-risk materials that might put the staff in danger, so they're ready to get us out at any moment."

Daniel nodded, refusing to give voice to the thread of suspicion that told him they'd be stuck at the lab longer than they anticipated.

BEN

Ben and Stephanie were quiet on the drive downtown. Every now and again, a police cruiser or ambulance with rotating lights and blaring sirens drove past the traffic. Obviously, Stephanie had noticed that something was up as well because she kept glancing ahead to see what was going on.

Car horns were blaring, and every so often, he noticed an angry driver standing with one foot out of his vehicle, arms spread, and yelling expletives at the ones in front of him.

"What the hell is going on out there?" Stephanie asked.

"Dunno. It might have something to do with that incident on Candlewood." Ben shrugged.

"This is insane. Traffic is never this bad in Witherton."

She was right. Witherton wasn't a huge city, but getting stuck in traffic was a rare occurrence. In fact, driving between the hours of 10 p.m. and 6 a.m., it often felt like being stuck in a ghost town. The urge to run a red light on an empty intersection was omnipresent during those hours, as if an invisible presence had sneaked into the car and whispered that it was okay to do so since nobody was around.

Ben got close to giving in to the temptation once. He had been sitting at the intersection of 13th Street and Church Street, scanning the intersection for signs of cops. When he was sure none were there, he gently pressed the gas pedal.

Even before the car eased forward, a Porsche buzzed past him without even slowing down while crossing the intersection. Blue and red lights appeared in Ben's rearview mirror. A cop car rolled after the Porsche, one that had been parked close to a restaurant behind Ben.

The Porsche driver had saved him a hefty ticket and taught him a valuable lesson—points on his driver's license weren't worth the twenty seconds he'd save to get home.

Stephanie slammed her palm against the center of the steering wheel. The car's horn shrieked, but the pickup in front of her didn't budge.

"Don't bother," Ben said. "It's completely backed up."

"I know, but... It's getting on my nerves."

"Why are you in such a rush?"

That was Ben's indirect way of asking *where are you going*.

"I'm not," Stephanie said. "I just hate being stuck in traffic."

The car moved forward, albeit inch by inch.

"Switch to the left lane." It's moving faster," Ben said.

"Yeah."

Stephanie rotated the wheel and got the nose of her car stuck between a jeep and Dodge in the left lane. The Dodge driver honked at Stephanie, but she ignored him and cut him off. Meanwhile, Ben was on his phone, checking the news. He was glad he wasn't the one driving the car because he would have gotten really angry.

The left lane moved a lot faster, and it soon became apparent why.

A few crashes had occurred, and the cars were parked in the right-hand lane with the owners standing outside and waiting for the police to arrive. Strangely enough, police drove right past the crashed vehicles.

Toward Candlewood Boulevard, maybe, Ben thought.

He entered his news app and almost let out a gasp at the bevy of news. Just then, a message appeared at the top of his screen. It was Melissa again.

Please come pick me up. There's something very wrong here.

"You okay?" Stephanie asked. "What's with the face? You look like you saw a ghost."

"Yeah. Um… Just gotta call Melissa. So, um…"

Would you mind being quiet?

"Right now?" Stephanie asked.

"Yeah. Something seems to be wrong at her work."

"Well, can't you wait until I drop you off?"

There it was. That jealousy. The first step that would inevitably ruin what they had because Stephanie would strive for more.

"Yes, now," Ben insisted. "So can you please just be quiet while I talk to her?"

"I'm not gonna be quiet in my own car so you can talk to your wife, who you're cheating on."

Ben gritted his teeth. Stephanie chose the worst time to act like a spoiled brat.

"Steph…"

"No. You know what? I'm sick of being a doormat for you."

So it began. Stephanie must have been holding those emotions bottled up for a long time. Who would have thought that something as stressful as being stuck in traffic would be the last drop?

"We can have this conversation if you like, but not right now," Ben said.

"Then when? Whenever I try to talk about this, you shut me out."

"I don't."

But that was a lie. He did, and he knew it. Stephanie never talked about the topic because Ben stubbed it before it could properly even bloom. He would quickly change the topic or shut her up by seducing her. By the time it was all over, Stephanie would give up on trying to open up the topic again.

But sitting inside the same car, stuck in traffic, she had Ben trapped. It almost made him wonder whether she'd planned it all along.

No, not Stephanie. That was beyond her intellectual and manipulative capabilities.

"If we're going to continue... whatever this is," She motioned in a circle between her and Ben, "then I need to know where we're standing."

Ben couldn't deal with this shit right now. The phone was in his hand, one tap away from calling Melissa. His wife. And this stranger in the car—because that's what she was, a stranger—was yelling at him, making demands.

"Fuck this," Ben said as he undid his seatbelt, opened the door, and stepped outside.

He caught a glimpse of shock and confusion crawling over Stephanie's face before it was replaced by anger. By the time she started shouting at him, he slammed the door shut, muffling her voice.

He didn't need to do that because the traffic around him was deafening anyway.

Ben dialed Melissa's number. After some time of silence, the call dropped. He tried a few more times, but the results were the same. He sent her a message: *What's happening? Are you okay?*

The message didn't go through.

"Shit."

He decided to send her a voice message. "Babe, I tried calling you, but the line's dead. Call me when you can, or text—"

A loud bang exploded from somewhere, interrupting Ben mid-sentence. He jerked his head toward the source of the sound. Whatever it was, it came from the direction where he and Stephanie were headed. He couldn't see what it was, though.

"Just call me when you get the chance, all right?" he finished recording the voice message and sent it to her.

He noticed people stepping out of vehicles and staring ahead. The words were incoherent, but their tones portrayed worry.

Ben turned his head to the tall buildings they were facing ahead to see a cloud of black smoke rising from the city into the air.

"Holy shit," he said.

A scream tore through the street nearby. A young man had climbed on top of a car's roof. Veins bulged on his neck as his head twitched left and right. The owner of the car was yelling at him to get the fuck off before he called the cops.

The man on the roof looked down at the driver before diving face-first at the man like a dog jumping to greet its owner. Ben could see the truculent expression on the driver's face morph into surprise as the man leaped toward him. Then, they were both out of sight behind the car.

What the hell?

More screaming, a cocktail of panic and shock. Nearby drivers held phones up to their ears, presumably calling 911.

Moments later, the man who had jumped on the driver shot up back into view. The screaming grew even louder then as people scrambled to get into their cars. Red liquid coated the man's chin and neck and dripped down to his V-neck sweater.

The man's head snapped from side to side. His lips pulled up into a snarl, revealing red ridges between teeth.

Blood. That's blood.

"Ben! Ben!" Stephanie was calling out to him.

At first, he hadn't heard her voice because of all the honking that pervaded the air. He swept his gaze back to her car to see her standing above, a look of worry on her face.

"Come back inside! Please!" she shouted.

At the sound of Stephanie's voice, the man with the blood on his chin swiveled in Ben's direction. Only four cars separated them. In that long moment, Ben wondered if those eyes were staring at him or something behind him. He was frozen, afraid that moving even by an inch could attract the man's attention.

The man broke into a feverish dash toward Ben.

Oh shit.

Ben ran back toward Stephanie's car. He vaguely became aware of the screams that filled the air. The man scrambled over the hood of the car in front of him, and it was only then that Ben noticed that his fingers were stained with blood, too, and they left imprints on the metallic surface of the vehicle.

Ben yanked open the door.

The man tripped and smashed his chin against the roof of the car he was climbing, but that didn't seem to dissuade him one bit.

Ben shoved the phone into the pocket of his pants and slithered inside the car. He slammed the door shut. Moments later, Stephanie was there with him, too.

The man had jumped from one car to another, and then another.

"Lock the door!" Ben shouted.

Stephanie pressed a button between the seats, and the distinct click of doors locking came from all sides of the car.

The man leaped off the roof of the jeep and right toward Stephanie's car. Instinctively, Ben raised his hands in defense. The front of the car dipped as the man landed on the hood. His hands and face pressed against the glass, smearing blood over it.

Strands of his hair were soaked in blood, too. At this proximity, Ben noticed how bloodshot his eyes were, almost to the point of the whites being completely gone.

"Oh my God!" Stephanie screamed.

The man pounded on the windshield. His fists produced squeaking sounds as they slid across the glass, further spreading blood over the windshield.

Stephanie let out a petulant scream as she repeatedly pressed the horn. It did nothing to stop the man from slamming his fist against the glass. Of course not. He was a man, not a cat. Either in panic or because she thought the outcome would be different, Stephanie kept hitting the horn with her palm.

But then, the man did stop, and his head snapped left so suddenly that spittle mixed with blood flew out of his mouth. He stared sheepishly at something then clambered up to his feet and ran in the direction of whatever he'd seen.

"Oh, Jesus! Oh, Jesus! Oh, Jesus!" Stephanie chanted. She turned her head to Ben and asked, "Ben, what do we do?"

Ben looked left and then right. There was some space between the cars in the right lane, enough for Stephanie's car to squeeze into. Then, she could climb onto the pedestrian walkway and bolt out of there.

"Turn right," he said.

"What?" she asked.

"I said turn right. Get between these two cars and then drive through the pedestrians' walkway."

"Are you serious? That's illegal! And not to mention the damage my car will suffer."

As if to answer her, something bumped into them from behind, sending their car a foot forward.

"Shit, what the fuck?!" Stephanie and Ben turned around to see the Dodge driver behind them holding his palm on the horn, his face contorted in a mixture of fear and impatience.

More and more people were running between cars. One sprinted past Stephanie's vehicle and broke the side rearview mirror clean off without even glancing behind at the damage.

"If you don't do it, we'll be stuck in here, and we might die!" Ben said.

"Okay! Okay!" Stephanie was hyperventilating.

She rotated the wheel then stepped on the gas pedal. The car lurched to the right. Ben's side of the door scraped loudly against the bumper of the BMW in front of them, which caused Stephanie to step on the brake. More angry honking ensued.

"Shit!" she shouted.

"Don't stop, Steph. Fuck them. Just keep going," Ben said.

Who gave a damn about some BMW driver? Lives were at stake here.

Stephanie listened to him. She slammed her foot on the gas, and the car produced another long *krrrt* as it further damaged the BMW. Even more angry honking.

"Keep going," Ben encouraged Stephanie.

The car painfully climbed on top of the walkway designed for pedestrians. Something directly underneath their seats scratched as the rear tires climbed as well.

"Good. Now keep driving, and get us off this fucking street," Ben said.

That proved more difficult than in theory. Panicked pedestrians ran in front of the car, forcing Stephanie to slow down every now and again.

"Come on! Get out of the way!" she shouted, intermittently pressing the horn to warn them.

Her side of the car scratched against the streetlight, rattling the entire vehicle.

"Fuck!" she screamed.

Right then, repairing the car was the last thing on Ben's mind. They just needed to get out of there because Melissa had been right. Something crazy was going on.

"Keep going. You're close, babe," Ben said.

He called her *babe* because he thought she could use some encouragement. The intersection was in view.

"Oh my God. If the cops pull us over…" she said.

"They won't. They've got bigger things to worry about."

Even when they turned right onto the perpendicular street, they weren't free of the traffic. But it was a lot sparser, so that gave Ben hope.

"Okay, you can get back on the road now." Ben pointed to the left.

"Hold on!" Stephanie said.

She jerked the wheel to the left. The car's front tires hit hard against the ground, then the rear ones, and then they were suddenly drifting smoothly on the road.

They were both breathing heavily, looking behind. It felt as though they'd outrun a tsunami.

Five minutes later, the traffic had become normal. Cars were still there, but not backed up or anxious like back on the other street.

"Jesus. What the hell was that?" Stephanie asked.

With adrenaline loosening its claws on them, Ben started to process everything that had happened just minutes prior.

"I don't know," he said.

He looked back, expecting to see the crazed man with blood on his chin running after their car. Just normal traffic, save for the occasional blare of a police siren.

"Let's just get as far away from downtown as we can," Ben said.

Krista

Krista barged inside the house with Nelson in her arms. Eric shut the door and locked it behind them.

"Did they follow us?" Krista asked, out of breath.

She knew the run from the driveway to the door couldn't have exhausted her so much. It was the panic taking its toll on her.

"No, I don't think so," Eric said. "We need to lock everything."

Krista gently lowered Nelson onto the couch and brushed the sweat from his forehead.

"I'll make sure all windows are closed and lower the blinds," Eric said. "And then I'm gonna get the car in the garage."

"With those people outside? Eric, it's dangerous. They could attack you," Krista said.

"We can't leave the car out there, honey. We might need it for a quick getaway."

Krista's throat closed up for a moment, disabling her from forming words.

A quick getaway. Those words didn't sit well with her. It implied that things would get so messed up they'd need to leave their home.

Things in the city were becoming crazy—that was for sure. It wasn't just some news exaggeration this time. Krista had seen it with her own eyes at the clinic and on the drive back home. People were breaking things, fighting…

No, fighting wasn't exactly the right word.

They were killing each other. Krista had never seen so much blood in her life. She was almost glad that Nelson was too sick because, if he looked out the window, it surely would have given him nightmares.

Krista looked down at Nelson. His eyes were closed, his chest rising and falling. Krista walked up to him and placed a hand on his forehead. He was burning up. It had been like this since last night. No matter what she tried, she couldn't bring the fever down.

It was starting to seriously worry her. Maybe he needed a day or two to get better, but the lack of a doctor's support made Krista feel vulnerable and helpless. She wasn't going to let that stop her, though.

She went into the bathroom and soaked a towel with cold water. She got some ice from the freezer and wrapped the towel around it.

She returned with the cold towel to Nelson and, kneeling in front of him, said, "Baby, this might get cold a little. But you have to keep it on, okay?"

Nelson responded with a soft moan. Krista gently lowered the icy towel over Nelson's forehead and wrapped it behind his head. He didn't protest or say anything.

"I'm going to get you some water. You have to drink, okay?"

She returned from the kitchen with a bottle of water. Nelson took two sips but refused to drink more.

"Baby, you have to drink," Krista said.

But Nelson looked like he wanted to sleep and be left alone. By then, Eric had lowered the blinds on all windows, which greatly dimmed the room, and went out into the garage.

Krista took Nelson's hand. It was burning hot. If she couldn't keep his fever down, she'd need to give him a tepid or cold shower. She knew that would result in a cat-in-a-bathtub kind of scenario, so she hoped it wouldn't have to come to that.

Outside, she heard the car starting up and the engine revving wildly. The sound traveled toward the garage where it crashed into something.

Oh God, Eric!

Krista ran into the garage, another wave of panic surfacing in her chest. She barged through the door to see the garage shutter lowering. Eric stood there, waving something in his hand at a person holding the door from lowering.

"Joe! Get the fuck off my property!" he shouted.

It took Krista a moment to realize that it was a wrench he was holding. The person trying to get inside was their neighbor, Joe, and he was in a hardly recognizable state.

His hair, which Eric always called "enviable" because of its blonde color and lushness, jutted in every direction. He frothed at the mouth as he hissed at Eric and snapped his teeth. His face jumped from one rigid expression to another, something Krista never thought him capable of.

For the seven years they'd known Joe, he and his husband Henry had always been polite neighbors. He helped them move their things in when they first bought the house, waved to them on his morning jog, and even came to express his condolences when he heard that Eric's dad had died a few years back.

But this Joe? The one with disheveled hair, an animalistic face, bloodshot eyes, and clothes stained with dirt? This was an entirely different person.

"Joe!" Krista shouted.

Joe's head snapped in her direction. She thought she'd see some recognition in those eyes, but she was wrong. There was something in there, but she couldn't place her finger on it. All she knew was that it terrified her.

The moment of distraction Krista had accidentally provided was enough for Eric to make the swing he'd been aiming for. The wrench produced a dull thud as it cracked against Joe's forehead. Joe's eyes rolled to the back of his head as he stumbled backward, releasing the garage door.

The shutter continued lowering. Joe produced a throaty growl as he dashed forward again, but it was too late. The door had closed then rattled as Joe's body slammed against it. Krista and Eric listened as the banging turned into scratching.

"Joe! I'm warning you!" Eric shouted.

The scratching continued.

"I'm going to call the cops!" Eric insisted.

"Eric, let's just go back into the house. Ignore him, and maybe he'll leave," Krista said.

Eric shot her a look, and she expected him to reprimand her. Instead, he nodded and said, "Yeah, you're right."

He cast a final glance at the garage door before he and Krista went back into the house. He locked the door leading to the garage even before Krista told him to do so. They both shared the same concern that Joe might somehow break in, even though the shutter was strong.

"Is Nelson okay?" Eric asked.

His voice sounded sonorous against the silence of the house.

"No. His fever is bad. I don't know what's going on." Krista was on the verge of crying again, but she suppressed that urge.

It was not the time for that. Plus, she wanted to make Eric feel like she was dependable, now more than ever.

Eric pulled out his phone, dialed a number, and pressed the phone to his ear.

"Who are you calling?" Krista asked.

"Ambulance," he said. A second later, he brought the phone down, frowning at it. "Line's dead."

"What? No, that can't be."

Krista tried calling with her phone, but the results were the same.

A part of Krista had believed until that moment that things would become better. That this was all just a scare that would be regulated soon. But with the phones dead, she understood just how serious this all had become.

"I'll make sure the rest of the house is secure. You tend to Nelson," Eric said.

Krista nodded.

Eric was about to leave but then returned and put a hand on Krista's cheek.

"Hey, we'll be okay, honey," he said in a soft voice.

Instantly, Krista's worries melted away because she knew Eric was telling the truth. There was a reason why she felt safe around him.

Still, as she turned on the TV and saw what was going on on the news, she couldn't help but worry that this was far bigger than what Eric could handle.

And it was still only in its infancy.

Boris Bacic

JAMES

James froze. His gaze was fixed on the draped window, his eyes desperately trying to perforate a hole in the curtains so he could see what was outside.

That sound from just before could have been anything. Why was the scream the first thing that came to James's mind?

Because that's what it was.

But maybe it wasn't. Now that James thought about it, it could have been anything. It could have been the sound of car tires; the sound of something scraping against something else. But there was too much vocality to it; that was what bothered James. It sounded too much like something made with human vocal cords, and not mechanical.

"Fuck," he said aloud, barely a whisper above the TV man's voice.

It was nothing, he tried to tell himself, but he couldn't pry his gaze away from the curtains. His door was equipped with a peephole, though. Why not use that, instead? He felt stupid for not thinking of it earlier.

James licked his lips and tip-toed to the front door, gently leaning his palms on it. He hated looking through peepholes. Ever since that one horror movie that he'd seen where the ghost almost jabbed the main character through the eye by inserting some sort of needle through the peephole, he had an irrational fear of that happening to him every time he looked.

The empty street came into view. The garage of his neighbor was still open. But even peeking left and right, James couldn't see anyone out there. He hadn't realized he was holding his breath until he pulled away from the peephole.

Whatever that sound was, it was no longer—

That same, clipped scream from before tore through the air again, this time much closer. It sounded like it was coming directly from outside the living room window. This was followed by a different scream—a masculine one—and then the patter of footsteps.

James was already pressed against the door once again, one eye closed, the other peeking through the peephole. He looked just in time to catch sight of a man running past his house, chased by a woman. And then, they were gone. The footsteps receded. A guttural gasp came from the street, and then a yelp, followed by silence.

It took James's brain a moment to process the image that he'd seen just now. The man had been dressed in a yellow uniform. The peephole made it impossible to discern any other features. The woman had been flailing her arms while running, her hair flying behind her.

No matter how much James strained to the side, he couldn't see the couple anymore. He had to know what was going on, so he did the only thing that he thought he could do.

He approached the window.

At first, he hesitated, his hand hovering just inches from the curtain. Planting one palm on the wall, he pinched the edge of the fabric between his forefinger and thumb. The motion made a wave run across the curtains.

Gingerly, James leaned as close as he could to the wall and pulled the curtain away, letting a sliver of gray light inside the house.

At first, all he saw was the empty street. That made him feel at ease. A part of him had been hoping that he wouldn't see those two. Ignorance really was bliss sometimes.

But then his eyes fell on the woman. He couldn't tell how he knew it was the same woman. His brain must have registered some detail that he hadn't actively thought about. Maybe the color of her clothes or the body language that she exhibited.

She was standing inside Sean's garage. The only reason why James saw her in the darkness of the interior was because of the glaring, yellow jacket. Darkness obscured most of her features, but James thought he could discern some of the details on her.

Her long hair was frayed and disheveled. A brown leaf was stuck on the back of her head. Dirt and dust covered her clothes as if she worked in construction. Her inner thighs were stained with a streak of something wet that trickled down to the bottom of her pant leg sleeves.

The woman stood crooked; one leg straight, the other slightly bent, her torso and head canted, her arms languidly hanging by her sides. Her shoulder twitched upward once, twice, like trying to shake off a persistent mosquito.

She must have been on drugs. There was no other explanation for such behavior. But what kind of drugs made a person go crazy like that? It wasn't unheard of, he knew that much. He'd heard of news like this happening from time to time, mostly in Florida.

His train of thought was interrupted when he noticed movement in the garage next to the woman. Something on the ground next to her. It was only then that James noticed the two feet on the floor of the garage, the toes pointing upward.

One foot feebly pulled back, the heel planted on the ground. The woman's head snapped in the direction of the movement so explosively that James's own neck produced a phantom twinge. Before he knew it, the woman was dropping to her knees in front of the person in the garage—James knew it was the man that was running just before.

Her hands were raised above her head. With a shrill cry, she brought her fists down on the person. The way the man was positioned, James couldn't see more than the feet, so the only indication that he had that the woman was hitting him was the fact that the man's feet jerked and twitched each time the woman fell on top of him.

The man's heels skidded across the ground with each hit, but that motion grew weaker and weaker with each passing moment. And then, the man stopped moving entirely, the only motion from him caused by the impact of the woman's fists.

She relentlessly pounded him while James watched in mute terror, his mind screaming something at him that he couldn't hear. His heart bounced against his ribcage, his hands trembling violently. A shaky gasp escaped his throat when the woman stood up and came into view again.

Her hands and sleeves were covered in blood. She continued standing just as she did before, her chin lowered toward the man on the floor.

James's eyes fixed on the feet of the man, trying to detect any kind of movement that would indicate that he was still alive. He had been transfixed on that so intently that he hadn't even realized that the woman was staring right at him when his eyes moved back up to her.

"Oh, shit!" James backpedaled from the curtain.

It fell back over the window, but the ripple didn't abate for a few moments longer. Footsteps resounded outside—a dash moving directly toward the house. The crash into the window that James braced himself for never came. No ghostly figure bursting through the glass and falling on the floor covered in curtains, only its outline visible as it scrambled to stand up,

Instead, there was silence.

James found his hands defensively raised in front of him. He lowered them, steadying his breath as much as he could. He refused to blink as he stared at the curtains, wondering if the woman had really seen him. He couldn't chase the image of her face out of his mind.

Against his better judgment, he took a step forward. The curtains were entirely still by then. James outstretched one hand. He didn't go for slow exposure this time. He scrunched a handful of the fabric in his hand and yanked it aside.

He screamed and jumped back when he did so. He had torn the curtain off a few rings, which left the window exposed just enough for him to get another detailed view on the window.

The woman's palms and forehead were pressed against the window, her quickened breaths fogging up the glass. Both her face and her fingers were caked in dirt and blood, which left smears on the window. Her broom-like hair fell across one eye. The exposed eye that stared back at James was bloodshot to the point of the whites being almost entirely replaced by red.

Her upper lip rose, revealing something green lodged between the chipped teeth. The grimace turned into something that was supposed to be a smile then curved into a snarl.

"Let in," she said, a single sentence that she went to repeat a few more times. "Let in. Let in. Let in. Let in."

A smile tugged at her lips, and then she let out a shrill, "Ha." Spittle flew from her mouth and sprayed the window. She pressed her cheek against the glass, smearing the blood and spit while never letting James out of her sight. The glass produced a squeaky sound, coupled with the hollow tapping of her broken fingernail.

James had had enough. He approached the curtains, grabbed them by the edge, and pulled them to cover the window.

"Let in. Let in. Let in," the woman repeated over and over.

James pressed his lips together tightly because he didn't trust himself not to shout back at the woman. And then, just as quickly as they started, all the sounds stopped. James breathed a sigh of tentative relief.

And then a knock came from the front door.

PIERCE

The air was electrified with tension. Voices barked orders from various directions while men in fatigues buzzed to and fro. There was something artificial about the whole atmosphere, Pierce realized. This outbreak was a huge problem, which meant a lot of pressure was placed on the top brass. No mistakes would be allowed.

"Captain Reynolds?" a voice next to the unit said. A lieutenant saluted Reynolds and said, "Sir. Right this way."

He spun on his heel and led the unit toward a cluster of erected tents.

"How are the defenses holding up?" Reynolds asked.

"So far, so good, sir," the lieutenant said. "No one's getting out unless we allow them to."

"Any patrols around the wider perimeter?"

"No need. We managed to get the walls up before this thing could spread."

Pierce saw the side of Reynolds's face contorting into a grimace. *Mistake*, that face said, but he chose to say nothing. That wasn't what they were here for.

"The general's waiting for you in there." The lieutenant stepped aside and gestured to one of the tents.

"Understood." Reynolds nodded and broke into a stride forward.

Pierce heard the raised voice even before he set foot inside the tent.

"I don't care how you do it. I want it done! You understand me?!"

"Yes, sir."

A large desk stood in the middle of the tent, a map of Witherton splayed over it. Various markers were placed around certain spots of the map.

A stocky man with snow-white hair and a uniform adorned with rows of flashy service ribbons was jabbing a finger at the chest of the major who stood stock still in front of him, spittle flying out of his mouth with each word he shouted. "And if you can't patch it up, I'm sending you personally down there to cement it. Got it?"

"Yes, sir." The major replied.

"Get the fuck out of here and handle it."

"Sir."

The major saluted the general and ran out of the tent without so much as glancing at Pierce and his teammates. The general placed his hands on his hips and stared down, worry accentuating the flabby ridges of his old face.

"General?" Reynolds said, which finally caught the man's attention.

"What do you want?" he snapped.

"We're Alpha Team. HQ sent us here."

"Alpha Team," the general echoed as if probing his memory to try and recall who the hell Alpha Team was and why HQ would send them. He threw one hand up then and said, "You're late, Alpha."

"Stopped for a smoke break. But looks to me like you guys are doing a good job handling this situation," Lincoln said.

The general shot Lincoln a venomous look. He looked about ready to catapult a whole volley of colorful insults at him.

"Can it, Lincoln," Reynolds said.

The unit was detached from regular military and, therefore, didn't answer directly to the general. Knowing this, Lincoln never passed up the opportunity to be sarcastic. Pierce wondered if he'd always been like that and, if so, how he managed to make it through boot camp in the first place.

The general's gaze lingered on Lincoln a moment longer as if contemplating whether to let his ironic remark slide.

"I take it you've been briefed on the situation?" he said, turning to the map.

"Just the basics," Reynolds said. "City's overrun by hostiles, and our mission is to rescue Doctor Kidman."

"They didn't give you the details?"

"No, sir."

The general leaned on the desk and closed his eyes. Another familiar facial expression Pierce had seen millions of times throughout his military career.

Those incompetent morons.

"You'll be going in through here." The general pointed to the eastern side of the wall. "Doctor Kidman is…" He traced a finger diagonally north and tapped the map. "…here."

"What's the place?" Reynolds asked.

"Welco Labs. Our satellite images showed Kidman entering the premises, but not leaving."

"When was the last time he was seen?"

"A day ago. We've spotted hostiles surrounding the building. You'll have to find a way inside. How you do it is completely up to you, captain."

"Why not send us in from the north side? Looks closer." Pierce pointed to the map.

"Place is crawling with hostiles," the general said. "You wouldn't make it ten feet without getting swarmed by them."

"How about a helicopter drop-off?" Shepherd suggested.

The general raised his eyebrows when he looked up at Shepherd, his brow furrowed like a shar-pei's. He looked surprised, but not in a good way, as if Shepherd's suggestion was the dumbest thing he'd heard in a while.

"And you are?" he asked.

"Corporal Shepherd, sir."

The general nodded. Pierce stared at the baffled expression on the old man's face until he realized: The general wasn't surprised by Shepherd's suggestion. He was surprised that a woman was sent on such an elite mission.

The old man didn't know Shepherd had survived some of the nastiest things in Afghanistan. She'd earned her place with Alpha Team just as much as Pierce or Lincoln or Murphy.

Pierce waited, expecting the general to ask Shepherd about her experience to confirm she was up to the mission.

Instead, the general said, "Helicopters are a no-go, corporal. Too much noise draws attention. Hostiles would be on you before you could get anywhere close to Doctor Kidman. A small strike team could move quickly and go undetected."

"Why's this doctor so important?" Murphy asked.

"He has all the data we need to synthesize a vaccine."

"Why is the military only now retrieving the data?" Reynolds frowned.

"This thing blindsided all of us. Hell, we didn't even know what it was until yesterday. When the outbreak started, Doctor Kidman tipped us off what it was, along with all the relevant data that confirms he's been working on a cure. Part of it, anyway."

"So now he wants us to rescue him in exchange for the data," Reynolds said.

"Yes. Captain, Doctor Kidman is invaluable if we want to end this. You have to get him back at all costs."

"And if he's dead?"

"Just the data, then. We'll have our scientists take over."

"Roger that. What's the intel on hostiles?"

The general walked over to a chair in the corner of the tent and picked up a folder that had been sitting atop it. He returned to the desk, opened the folder, and tossed the photographs that were inside it over the map.

Some were satellite images of Witherton showing people scrambling down the streets in random directions while being chased. Others were close-up shots of victims. And then there were photographs of the infected.

"Those are some hard-ass drugs," Lincoln joked, pointing to a picture of the infected with bloodshot eyes and an arm missing from the shoulder socket.

"Guy looks like he doesn't care he just lost an entire arm," Murphy said.

Sure enough, it was like that. People who had been mutilated like that would either fall unconscious due to the shock or scream in pain, their faces contorted into agonizing grimaces. The infected in the picture looked angry.

"That's because he doesn't." The general put his hands behind his back. "The intel we have on the hostiles is still inconsistent. We still don't know enough about them. They move like a herd, and they seem to be coordinated about attacking the non-infected. They scream to draw attention when they see a target, and they're extremely violent."

"So, they're like zombies, essentially," Lincoln said.

"They're more dangerous than zombies. They're very aggressive. They can run, and they don't stop attacking until they're dead. Not very smart, though, so you at least don't need to worry about that. I don't need to mention you're authorized to shoot on sight. Just be ready to haul asses out of there because gunshots are sure to attract more of them."

"What about survivors?" Pierce asked.

For the briefest moment, the image of his mother flashed through his head as he remembered her, a slim woman in her thirties. She would have been much different now, perhaps even unrecognizable by her own son.

"Not your concern," the general said. "Try to stay out of their way, but if you determine they're a threat to the mission, you're authorized to neutralize them."

"Anything else we should know?" Reynolds asked.

"One more thing. Once you're inside, there's no going back until the mission is complete. The ropes you'll be using to climb down will be retracted, and you'll be stuck in the city. HQ will keep in touch with you, but their support will be limited. Once you've found Doctor Kidman, signal us from the rooftop, and we'll send in a chopper for evac. Make sure your team understands this, Captain Reynolds."

Murphy's words echoed in Pierce's mind. *We're going on a suicide mission.*

"All right," Reynolds said. "No time to waste. Alpha, move out."

"The lieutenant will lead you to the entrance. We're all counting on you and your team, captain," the general said.

Alpha left the tent. The same lieutenant who led them to the tent when they touched down was waiting for them in front.

"Follow me," he said.

They walked in silence, which didn't last long before Lincoln spoke up, "You notice how irritable the general was? He needs a visit to a proctologist to get that stick out of his ass."

"Imagine if you were in charge for an outbreak of this scale," Shepherd said. "If anyone under him fucks up, it'll be his ass on the line."

"Probably a good time to consider retirement options."

"He was eyeballing you, Shepherd," Pierce said.

"Gross." Shepherd wrinkled her nose.

"Not for the reasons you think," Lincoln added. "He's an old man. Probably wondering: What's a woman doing on military missions instead of cooking her husband's meal and looking after the kids at home."

"Can the chatter," Reynolds, always the strict, serious leader, said. "We got an important mission to complete, so stay focused. Got it?"

A few reluctant yeses came from the team.

"Over there." The lieutenant pointed to a tall ladder leading to the top of the wall.

"Hope none of you are afraid of heights," Lincoln said as he set his foot on the first rung.

A soldier was waiting for them at the top of the wall. He was talking to Reynolds, but Pierce wasn't listening because he was overlooking the town. It was the first time he got a better view, and not through a thick window of the military helicopter.

The smells were the first thing he noticed because they were so numerous and he needed a moment to identify each of them.

They were smells of stale blood, malady, death, and grief, but there was also a whiff of smoke, fire, and cinders. The stench of a city on its last legs.

But it wasn't just Pierce's sense of smell that was saturated.

He scanned the streets under the tall walls. Corpses interspersed the roads, often in piles, drizzled with streaks and splotches of red like an abstract piece of artwork. Pierce couldn't see it from here, but he imagined flies buzzing around fresh and old corpses alike, the limbs of the dead bodies stiff with rigor mortis, a pungent smell of rotten eggs emanating from them.

Black smoke rose from the city into the sky, a sure sign that a fire was burning somewhere.

Distinct *pop-pop-pop* sounds occasionally ripped through the air, along with police sirens that wailed sadly in the distance as if they themselves were crying for help.

There some other sound there, far off in the distance but impossible to focus on. The harder Pierce tried to place it, the more it seemed to elude him just enough to make him wonder whether the bevy of noise was making him imagine things.

It was there, though. And the winds that howled through the city carried with them the faintest screams of dying people.

"We'll cover you. Once you're down, we're pulling the rope back up," the soldier on the wall said, pointing to the rope hanging off the side.

Reynolds gave him a curt nod then turned to his unit and jutted his head toward the rope. Murphy was the first one to undertake the descent. He rappelled down the wall with fluidity, and once he touched ground, the stock of his firearm was against his shoulder as he scanned the perimeter for danger.

Lincoln went next, then Shepherd, Pierce right after her. He didn't think about the danger or the possibility of dying as he lowered himself deeper and deeper into the city with each kick of his boots against the wall.

Soldiers had an amazing ability to block certain things from entering their minds. It helped them keep a cool head, save teammates, and complete missions. The illusion of being safe, invincible even, was always present until it wasn't. It was necessary.

A panicked soldier was a dead soldier

Reynolds came down last.

"Move out," he said.

Pierce resisted the urge to look behind at the rope spooling on the ground because he didn't want to see it getting reeled out of his reach. His peripheral vision caught a pile of dead bodies on the shoulder of the road. He refused to look at that, too.

They were officially inside the infected city, and Pierce couldn't shake the feeling that they'd just descended the rope into a well full of snakes.

Boris Bacic

BEN

Stephanie drove slowly as she and Ben observed the mess in the city.

Shop windows were broken, trash littered the streets, and…

"Oh my God. Is that a dead body?" Stephanie asked.

A woman was splayed in the middle of the street, face-down. A pool of blood spread around her head like a morbid halo. The cars that drove in front of Ben and Stephanie gave the dead body a wide berth. No one stopped to see if she needed help (which she obviously did), or to call an ambulance.

Not like they'd be able to, anyway. Phones were busy, and even emergency services were unavailable.

Stephanie significantly slowed down and peeked out the window as she drove past the dead body. Deducing whether the woman was dead or not wouldn't change anything, and yet, human nature couldn't resist a peek at a gruesome scene.

Maybe the taste for the macabre helped the person feel more alive. Maybe it was just juvenile curiosity, like discovering masturbation.

"Oh God. She *is* dead," Stephanie said.

"Just keep driving," Ben said.

He glanced at his phone a few times, hoping to see a message from Melissa. Nothing. Defeated, he put the phone back into his pocket and changed the staticky radio station. Previously, some pop music played inside the car. Neither he nor Stephanie noticed when the music in the car went mute.

First, he heard a low voice punctuated by the hiss of the bad frequency. Then, it cleared up enough to understand what the voice was saying. He turned up the radio.

"...keep the public informed as soon as they have more information. Our insiders believe this is a terrorist attack on Witherton to—"

Ben changed the station.

"...authorities. Roads leading into all the northern parts of Witherton are backed up. We've already received reports of over twenty-five crashes—"

He changed the station again.

"People are apparently going crazy and violently attacking anyone in sight. Reports indicate that one person jumped on a woman and ripped her throat out. In my fifteen years of working as a journalist, I've never—"

"...military personnel moving throughout the city. Panic is high among the citizens—"

"...just in. A group of individuals who police describe as "dangerous men on drugs" crashed into a jewelry store on Main Street and violently murdered the employee working there. When police arrived, they, too, were attacked. Civilians have been ordered to—"

"...course of action is to stay inside, lock your doors, and cover your windows. The military is already involved in containing the matter and—"

He shut the radio off.

"Fucking hell," Ben said. "The hell is going on?"

"I don't know, but I'm scared, Ben," Stephanie said.

He avoided looking at her. She didn't seriously expect him to prioritize her safety in this mess, did she?

"What were you gonna do downtown, anyway?" he asked, not caring about her having the upper hand anymore.

"All I wanted to do was get some gluten-free products."

"That's it?"

"Yeah."

"Then why did you get all ready like you're going out on a date?"

Stephanie let out a nervous chuckle. "Jealous?"

"No. Is that how you were trying to make me feel?"

She swallowed. "So, what do we do now?"

"Now, you drive me home so I can pick up my wife."

Stephanie snapped at Ben in a surprised leer. "Are you serious?"

"Do I look like I'm joking?"

"Ben, do you not see the state of the city?" Stephanie gestured to the street in obvious chaos. "Even if we make it to your place, there's no way we'll get all the way to Welco Labs."

"We?" Ben cocked an eyebrow.

Stephanie opened and closed her mouth, perhaps thinking of what to say next. "I'm sorry?"

"Look, I appreciate your concern, but Melissa is my wife. I need to go find her." Before Stephanie could ask *what about me*, Ben added, "You should drive back home after you drop me off. If you use South Street, you should be able to get back without any issues."

"So, that's it, huh? You're just going to throw me away like a used dish rag because things are getting heated up?" she asked.

Ben was fed up with Stephanie's bratty behavior. It was in moments like those that he understood she was not wife material and wouldn't be for some time. He liked being with her for the sex, but that was it.

He wished that Melissa had one trait that Stephanie harbored. His wife was loving, smart, mature, but his mother had been right all along. If things didn't work in the bedroom, they wouldn't work anywhere else. So rather than look for a reason to pick fights with Melissa, he went behind her back and found someone who could perform the duties she didn't.

But Ben wasn't a cheater. Cheating implied not being satisfied with what you had at home. Ben was perfectly content with the woman he had at home. He was just missing one small piece of the puzzle. And that's where Stephanie stepped in.

But it was all becoming too much for him. He hadn't agreed to deal with her drama and offer emotional support. They were supposed to be a fling and nothing more. If Stephanie was going to try and make it more than that, then Ben would have no choice but to end things with her.

Really a shame because she fucked like a wild animal, and she and Ben were sexually compatible as if it was something written in the stars. Finding a substitute for her would be difficult.

"I made things clear where we stand when we started dating. I'm not going to have this discussion with you now," Ben said, and that should have made it more than clear to Stephanie that the topic was closed.

She was facing forward, but her eyes were unfocused, shimmering with a sadness he never saw her express. "I know. I just thought…"

"What?"

"Never mind."

I thought you cared about me. I thought you loved me. She wanted to say something down those lines, he assumed.

"Okay," he said, deciding not to play her game.

Still, he expected some sort of defiance from her. She faced forward, gripped the steering wheel with both hands, and said, "Fine."

Fine. Such a cold and atonal voice. Almost as if she didn't care. Except she did. Ben heard it in the microscopic crack that seeped out of the word,

Stephanie pulled the car over to the shoulder of the road.

"What are you doing?" Ben asked.

Stephanie turned the key to kill the engine. She undid her seatbelt and said, "I need to visit the pharmacy. I'll be right back."

"Wait," Ben said as Stephanie's hand reached for the door handle. She paused and looked back at him, wearing a hopeful expression. "It might be dangerous. I'm coming with you."

He liked seeing the reinforced hope on her face. It made him realize that things were not over between him and Stephanie. Not by a long shot.

Whenever he was too good to her, she became more daring. That was why he shot her down from time to time before helping her back up. It was a fluctuating ride, their affair.

As they stepped out of the car and crossed the street toward the pharmacy, Ben found himself wondering whether Melissa was okay. He found himself feeling strangely indifferent about her well-being, and that worried him.

HEATHER

There were often moments when Heather thought about how much better her life would have been if Abby didn't exist. She used to be ashamed of fantasizing about that, but one can live in denial for only so long before they need to face the truth.

As a twelve-year-old, Heather had been excited to get a sister. She remembered the day her mom returned from the hospital with something tiny wrapped in a bundle in her arms. Heather danced around her mom, shouting, "I wanna see! I wanna see!"

Her mom showed her little Abby. Only her head was poking out of the blanket. Her eyes were closed, but her mouth opened, and she let out a tiny cough, which turned into crying. Heather thought she was the most beautiful thing ever.

That feeling was only a distant memory, a fading echo in the mountain. What remained was resentment and constant annoyance.

Heather wouldn't have been in this situation if Abby didn't exist. She would have gone to college somewhere outside Witherton. She'd only need to visit during the breaks, and the lack of constant dealing with Abby wouldn't have frayed their relationship to how it was now.

She would have met a nice guy at college, just like all the other girls, and she'd have lots of friends there.

Heather often liked to fantasize about the life she was missing out on. It was usually during the few minutes of silence she managed to grab before either Abby or a demanding customer from Wonder Meal called out to her as if to remind her where she belonged.

Instead of the bright life she yearned for, she was stuck in a city she hated, taking care of her sister while putting her future on hold.

"Heather?" Abby's voice broke the silence in the apartment, proving Heather's point about not having peace even to fantasize.

It was a little past 7 a.m. Heather went to bed late, fell asleep even later, and woke up early.

"Yes?" Heather asked.

"I'm hungry," Abby said.

She hadn't eaten dinner the night prior. After Heather slapped her, Abby had run off into her room and hadn't come out until morning. Heather was just glad Abby forgot about the slap because the last thing she wanted was to have to worry about that on top of everything else.

"Okay. What would you like to eat?" Heather asked, but she already knew the answer.

"Cereals," Abby said.

Abby always had cereals for breakfast, but they had to be made in a specific way: Take out the bowl, pour the cereal in first, then pour the milk over them in circular motions so that they get soaked properly, and finally, sprinkle a little bit of cinnamon on top.

"Here you go." Heather served the bowl to Abby.

"Thank you, Sis. You're the best," Abby said.

You're the best. It's what she said, not just to express gratitude but also love. Heather had stopped telling Abby that she loved her a long, long time ago. The best she gave her nowadays was, "Nice work." Abby, seeing Heather as a role model, said similar things.

That was how *you're the best* came to be the new *I love you.*

Abby's politeness only made Heather feel guilty about slapping her and about wishing earlier for Abby to not have been born.

While Abby ate, Heather checked the internet again. Still not working, much to her dismay. Turning on the TV, she discovered even the emergency broadcast that repeated itself on the screen was gone. That was when a terrifying thought hit Heather.

Oh God, what if this isn't happening just in Witherton? What if it's the entire world?

Heather ran a hand through her hair, thinking about the likelihood of the entire country being toppled by... whatever was happening out there.

She had been so nerve-wracked that she hadn't had time to consider what exactly might have been causing all of this. She knew people out there were acting crazy and violent, but that was it.

Yet, if this thing was a disease of some sort and it spread beyond Witherton, then they would have been waiting for a rescue that would never come. If the big cities got hit, it made sense that the government would prioritize saving those places first, leaving shitholes like Witherton on the back burner.

Heather looked at Abby, considering her options. Her sister was crunching cereals at the kitchen table. If she left to look for a way out of the city, she would need to bring Abby with her.

Or would she?

She wouldn't feel safe dragging her around with all the crazy stuff happening out there. Hell, she wouldn't even feel safe going out there by herself, but it would be easier to worry only about her own safety rather than two people.

However, she couldn't leave Abby alone here, either. What if something happened to Heather while she was gone? Abby would be waiting for her to return; food would run out, and then?

Would she wander out into the streets to be killed by the red-eyed people, or would she remain in the apartment, starving and hoping for her sister to return?

What am I supposed to do?

The emotion of hate once again wiggled into her spine. Her parents should have been here. They would have known what to do. Heather would have felt so much safer with her mom and dad taking control of the situation.

If Dad said they were waiting for rescue, then that was what they were doing, and not a shred of doubt would exist in Heather's mind. If he said they were leaving, Heather knew she'd have no need to fear the red-eyed people because her dad would do everything to protect the family.

Just give me a sign or something, tell me what to do. Please.

She felt like crying again. An accumulation of emotions, and not just worry over the red-eyed people outbreak.

Then, she received the sign she had been looking for.

Her phone vibrated in her pocket. She pulled it out so quickly that she almost dropped it on the ground. A message stood at the top of the screen with EMERGENCY ALERT plastered in big letters. Heather opened it, and her eyes darted across the message.

"Military checkpoints," she said. "They're organizing military checkpoints."

Abby gave her a look of confusion. A trickle of milk slid down her lower lip.

Heather read the message one more time, looking at all the places where military checkpoints were being organized. The closest one to Baldwin was a few miles away, just past St. Peter. They could make it there today, but they needed to go immediately because other people would most likely want to go there, too.

But why were they organizing military checkpoints and not a rescue? Maybe it was still too dangerous for rescue services to enter the city, so they were willing to meet the citizens halfway there.

Hope bloomed in Heather's chest. It was going to be a dangerous road, but it was better than waiting for something to happen.

"Sis, can we do the puzzle again?" Abby asked.

Looking down at her sister, Heather realized just how dangerous the road ahead might be. If Abby so much as started crying, it could attract unwanted attention. That was why she'd need to make sure Abby was as comfortable as she could get.

It was only a few miles.

"No, Abby. We can't."

"Why not?"

"Get dressed when you're done eating. We're going outside."

KRISTA

Krista and her family remained cooped up in the house, waiting for any news of rescue. The neighborhood had fallen quiet, but it was a bad kind of silence, one meant to lull a person into a false sense of safety. In truth, as soon as they stepped outside, they'd become targets.

Nelson wasn't getting any better. The fever refused to subside, even with an icy shower. Medicine did nothing to help him, either.

What worried Krista the most was the fact that he hardly remained awake. The only time he woke up was to mumble a word or two before falling back asleep. He hardly ate or drank.

"We can't stay here any longer, Eric. Nelson needs help," Krista said.

"I know," Eric retorted.

It felt like the thousandth time that they'd had this conversation in the past two days.

They were sitting at the kitchen table, listening to the wall clock ticking away. The air in the house was heavy with trepidation. Although Eric didn't say it, Krista could see the fear in his eyes.

He, too, feared that they would go to check on Nelson and find that he had no pulse. And at the rate at which his condition was worsening, that was bound to happen.

"Eric, I'm scared," Krista said. "What if he doesn't get better? What if he…"

What if he dies, she wanted to say but couldn't bring herself to do so.

Eric reached across the table and took Krista's hand. "He won't. I won't let it happen."

Krista was past the point of crying. She felt numb, and that scared her even more. What if Nelson really did end up dying and she remained numb for days, weeks, or maybe even months before the emotions finally hit her?

Don't think about death. Nelson is going to be okay. It's just a fever.

A fever that refused to go down. It wasn't a normal fever. And it just came out of nowhere.

What worried Krista the most about that whole thing was what they kept mentioning on the news: Outbreak. She didn't like that word. An outbreak implied a contagious disease, which meant Nelson might have contracted something and that was why he was having a fever.

The news was talking about an entirely different kind of outbreak, though. The outbreak in Witherton caused people to go crazy and violent. Krista had seen the footage. People with bloodshot eyes—just like Joe's had been—attacking other people, angrier than anything Krista had ever seen before.

But that wasn't Nelson. Nelson only had a fever.

Still, the word "outbreak" on the news made her paranoid enough to check Nelson's eyes and make sure they weren't red. She stopped watching the news after that.

"Then, what are we going to do? We can't stay here and hope he gets better. We have to get him help," Krista said.

"I know. And you're right. We can't stay here. But we can't go out, either. You saw what happened out there."

Eric didn't need to remind her of it. The image was already deeply embedded in her mind.

After closing the garage door on him, Joe remained motionless in the street in front of their house for over a day. Eric had watched him, and he confirmed that he hadn't budged from that one spot at all.

When Krista looked through the peephole, she saw Joe standing with one shoulder slightly slanted, head twitching every so often. Something was wrong with him, and despite the need to go out and ask Joe if he was okay, something inside Krista screamed that it would be a terrible idea.

Her assumption proved true only hours later when she heard a scream from the foyer. She had been in Nelson's room, checking his temperature when it happened. She ran downstairs, worried that Eric might have gotten injured, or that Joe had somehow broken inside the house.

She found Eric standing a few feet from the door, his chest heaving up and down, eyes unblinking in terror. She had asked him what was wrong. He couldn't speak. When Krista looked through the peephole, Joe was no longer there.

That had unnerved her a lot more than seeing him standing motionless in one spot. While disturbing to see him that way, she at least had her eyes on him. But with Joe no longer in front of the house, he could be anywhere. He could be standing pressed against their window, peeking into the parts of the living room not covered by the blinds.

Eric needed a minute to compose himself, and then he told Krista what had happened. One of their neighbors had approached Joe from behind to try and talk to him. Apparently, Joe had remained unresponsive until the neighbor put a hand on his shoulder.

That was when Joe lunged at the neighbor. He bit his ear off, forcing the neighbor into a run. Joe dashed after him. Eric had no idea whether the neighbor managed to get away or not.

Krista was surprised she didn't hear any screaming in the street since Nelson's window faced the front of the house.

"Which neighbor was this?" she'd asked Eric.

"The vet that lives on the cul-de-sac."

"Well, why didn't you let him in? Eric, he could have helped Nelson."

Krista wasn't expressing herself nearly how she wanted to. She wanted to call Eric an idiot and shout at him for not opening the door. His response was a raised eyebrow that furrowed his forehead all the way to the bald scalp.

"A veterinarian could help Nelson?" Eric asked.

It made Krista feel stupid, which instantly pacified her anger toward her husband.

"I'm just saying he could have used the help. And so could we," she said because she refused to bow her head down.

"I'm not going to risk your and Nelson's lives. You saw what Joe is like."

There was slight impatience in his tone. It was rare to see Eric like this, which meant that the whole situation must have been getting to him, too, no matter how stout his personality seemed sometimes on the outside.

"Yeah, but there's three of us and one of him. We could have…"

"Honey," he interrupted. "I hit him in the face with a wrench, and he just kept running right back at us. There's no way I could stop him."

Eric had a point. Krista hated agreeing with him, not because it made him right but because it felt like admitting that they were helpless.

"But if we can't go out, what are we going to do?" Krista asked.

Eric pulled his hand away and leaned in the chair. He took a deep breath through his nose then exhaled, staring into empty space. Whatever he was contemplating, it wasn't going to be anything good. It would involve either something extremely risky or something that would prolong the feeling of helplessness.

Or maybe it would be both.

When Eric looked at Krista, she knew exactly what he was going to suggest. After years of being married, she could read his every eye contact, every subtle shift of the body language. Plus, she'd learn what kind of problem-solving he preferred.

She didn't like it because she realized how wrong she had been.

Eric's solution wouldn't involve either a risk or that feeling of helplessness while waiting for something to happen. It would involve both.

"Tomorrow morning, I'm going out there to look for help," he said.

JAMES

James's head snapped to the door.

Did I lock it did I lock it did I lock it.

In his panic, he thought he'd see the doorknob twisting, which would be followed by the latch clicking out of place and the door creaking open. But then he remembered that he actually had locked the door earlier.

Three soft raps resounded on the door. James blinked, his eyes stinging from staring wide-eyed for so long. The entire thing felt so surreal that he had the urge to pinch himself just to make sure he wasn't stuck in a nightmare.

Knock, knock.

Two knocks this time as soft as before.

James found himself tiptoeing toward the door. The TV man in the background was too loud, too distracting.

Stop talking so loudly, James thought to himself. Sounds often impaired his other senses, like vision. Often when he needed to find the spot where his GPS was leading him, he needed to turn down the music in his car in order to focus better.

When he approached the door, the fear of getting jabbed through the eye intensified more than before. He aligned his eye with the peephole and stifled a scream that threatened to escape his throat.

A smiling face stared back at him, too close to the peephole. Although the peephole distorted the face—gave it a large forehead and a long nose—there was no mistaking that the man standing in front of the door was the same one that had been running just moments ago.

James had to clamp a hand over his mouth to suppress his breathing. A rivulet of blood went from the man's forehead down the side of his face. His receding hair was sticky with red. When his head twitched, James realized that it wasn't just the peephole that made his nose look twisted. His nose actually was crooked as if broken.

It was only then that James figured that the smile on the man's face wasn't a smile at all. It was a rictus. Before looking, James had been sure that it was the woman knocking on the door because... who else could it be?

But the glassy *tap, tap, tap, tap* coming from the window assured him that she was still very much here, still very much aware of his presence. Then came the knocking again. And then both sounds overlapped.

James stepped away from the door, his eyes darting from it to the window.

"Let in," the woman said, her voice garbled by the phlegm in her throat.

"In. In," a deeper voice at the door said.

"Let in. Let. Let."

"In. In. In."

"Leave me alone!" James realized that he was shouting those words only after they were out.

The house went silent. Even the TV man had stopped speaking. And then the *tap, tap, tap* and *knock, knock, knock* continued.

Only now they weren't just coming from the window and the door. They were coming from the walls of the house. James traced the sound with his eyes as it slid across the wall, intermittently going from a knock to a scratch. They ended up in the kitchen where they turned into more glassy taps.

The backdoor!

James rushed into the kitchen. This time, he didn't bother stifling his scream when he saw the face of the woman pressed against his kitchen window. She was staring at him, her fingernails gently raking the glass.

James ran to the door to find it locked tight. The woman didn't even bother trying to go for it. Instead, she continued staring at James with those wide, bloodshot eyes, her mouth making bubbles as she pressed her cheek against the glass.

The lack of curtains and blinds in the kitchen made James feel vulnerable. The only thing he could do was leave the room, so that was what he did. Just as he reached the threshold, a bang came from the window, rattling the frame.

He spun around to see the woman slamming her palm against the window, slowly, gently, but steadily, as if to tell him that she was coming inside sooner or later. James closed the door between the living room and the kitchen and locked it before rushing upstairs to his bedroom.

Looking outside the window at the desolate street, he couldn't see anyone. The silence upstairs unnerved him even more than the noise that those two people were making.

James fished out his cell phone and dialed 911. The call dropped almost immediately. Calling for help was a no-go it seemed.

He sat on the bed and exhaled. He hadn't realized how exhausted he was until then. He knew that he should find an object that he could use as a defense weapon, but he didn't have anything in his bedroom, and he sure as hell wasn't going to go down into the kitchen again.

James closed his eyes, wondering what the hell was happening. The silence that filled the house made him wonder if the "guests" outside had already left. But every time he thought that, a sound would come from downstairs.

A single tap or a knock, just enough to remind him that they were still here. And that they had no intention of leaving.

***

James couldn't tell how long he had been sitting in his bedroom. The clock on his phone told him that it was a little past six. *There goes my day off.*

The urge for a cigarette was strong. His cigs and lighter weren't in his pocket, though, which meant that he must have left them down in the living room at some point. He still wasn't craving nicotine enough to actually go downstairs to retrieve them.

He had tried calling the police a few more times, but there was no response. He had texted Julie again, but the message couldn't be delivered. He was tempted to lie down, but his eyes kept flitting to the open bedroom door, his ears straining to hear any sounds that were coming from downstairs.

Staring out the window, he contemplated using the second-floor awning to escape to his neighbor's house— or elsewhere. But every time that thought occurred to him, he remembered how that woman had chased down the man. She had been running so fast after him, and James was not a man who did any cardio—at all. That, coupled with the fact that he smoked, rendered him incapable of any prolonged physical activities that required the use of oxygen.

It was growing dark outside, and there was no indication that things would be resolved by the end of the day. A big part of James was hoping that he would receive further news from the government soon or maybe hear vehicles outside—military trucks going from house to house to rescue civilians.

With the sun slowly saying its goodbye for the day, James started to realize that maybe this was going to take much longer than he initially thought.

Lock your doors. Cover your windows. Avoid making too much noise.

James had already broken two out of the three rules. Did that mean he was already a dead man?

With nothing but time on his hands, he began to question what was making those people behave like that. She definitely looked like a drug addict, but if it were drugs, then the case would have been isolated to one person.

This was something different. Maybe one of those conspiracy theory groups was right. Something in the food or water or air that was making people go crazy like that.

James stood up because he was becoming too restless. He looked out the window again before deciding it was time to go downstairs. He told himself that it was important in order to assess the situation, but inhaling smoke into his lungs was really the thing that was on his mind.

He tiptoed downstairs, gently putting one foot below the other, his neck craning to get a better look into the living room. The intruder that he expected to see standing in the middle of the room was not there.

James's eyes fervently scanned to see if anything was out of place. The red glow of the screen was still on, but the TV man had stopped speaking entirely. Things in the room seemed exactly how he had left them, which made him exhale a quiet sigh of relief.

His eyes fell on the Marlboro pack sitting in the middle of the coffee table, right next to the lighter. It was a short distance to cross. Barely ten feet. But James would need to walk next to the front door in order to reach it. He stared at the wooden doorframe, wondering if the man was still on the other side.

Only one way to find out.

James held his breath as he sneaked toward the door. His ankle cracked at the worst possible time. He stopped momentarily just to see if he would get a reaction from the door.

Nothing.

That encouraged him to draw closer to it. Once he was in front of it, he leaned and peeked through the peephole for what felt like the millionth time that day.

The face that he anticipated to greet him wasn't there, but James was far from relieved. The man in the yellow uniform stood at James's doorstep, facing away from the door this time, his shoulders and head slouching.

James thought he could see his back rising and falling in irregular patterns of breathing. Then, without any indication, the man's head twitched sideways, revealing the side of his face that was covered in blood. He farther spun until he was facing the door, but he was staring somewhere above, his mouth agape.

Not wanting to wait and see what had caught his attention, James stepped away from the door. He shuffled to the coffee table, his eyes remaining glued to the door. He outstretched one hand sideways to grab the cigarettes, but his hand clawed thin air instead.

He had to look where the table was in order to take hold of the pack and lighter. The moment he did that, a sound—a different and louder one—ripped outside his house.

***

It was a shout, a feminine one. Not a shriek like the one that James had heard a few hours ago. No, this was a voice riddled with fear as it shouted an imperceptible word to another person. It was preceded by silence and then it shouted once more.

"Come on!" the voice said.

James was filled with both dread and hope. Another *normal* human was out there, but they were obviously in trouble.

This time, James didn't bother tiptoeing to the peephole. He practically ran into the door as he looked outside yet again. He arrived just in time to see the yellow-uniformed man running out into the street. His head swiveled left and right, and then his eyes locked with something that James couldn't see. He opened his mouth to let out a blood-curdling scream and then ran out of view.

"Shit!" James hissed.

He ran to the window and moved the drapes, not caring that the woman might be there still. She wasn't.

"Don't stop!" the feminine voice said once more.

That was when the person finally came into view. A woman with a backpack over her back and an ax in her hands was stumbling down the street. She looked back, and a man in a suit came into view, running after her, his cheeks puffing and deflating as he ran behind her.

The scream coming from the yellow-uniformed man caught the woman's attention. It was too late, though, James realized. The man was already bull-rushing her, and he was going to tackle her to the ground and then beat her to a pulp.

But the woman was faster. One swipe of her ax, and the man was kissing the ground. It had happened so fast that James couldn't register what she did to the man.

However, when the man's head rose, his cheek had been split open so badly that the entire lower row of his teeth was visible. Yet, he was already standing up, his eyes fixed on the woman; not in anger or vengeance but with a hunger that James couldn't explain.

The woman never gave him a chance. She kicked him so hard in the face that the man rolled over to his back.

"Angela, we gotta move! More of them are coming!" the man in the suit said as his head jerked in various directions.

Just then, screams filled the air. They seemed to come from everywhere, and they were so loud that James was compelled to look back just to make sure no one was inside his house.

But he had to help these people. There was no way he could leave them to die there. He didn't know how he knew they were in mortal danger, but, for some reason, he knew that if he didn't intervene, two corpses would litter his view of the street.

He found himself unlocking the door before he even processed the thought properly. Then, fresh air hit him square in the face as he opened the door and stepped outside.

"Over here!" he shouted and waved the two people over.

Their eyes fell on him. For a moment, James thought he recognized hesitation in the woman's eyes. As if she weighed whether to trust him or not. The moment was over just as quickly as it started, and the two strangers were running toward James, his invitation accepted.

The woman who had been at James's window was running closely behind them. And she was catching up to them.

James opened his mouth to warn the man in the suit, but it was too late. The woman had already tackled him. He fell forward, his palms outstretched in front of him to soften the fall. The woman was clawing at his back, climbing higher and higher on top of him. The man screamed and shouted something that James couldn't understand.

The lady with the ax had noticed the entire thing, and she was already rushing to help her friend. She swung the ax backward and then batted. The blade of the ax lodged itself into the neck of the woman, whose face instantly went slack.

Holy shit!

When the ax was pulled out, a thick, horizontal line of red appeared on her neck. Then, blood began gushing out like a fountain, and the woman fell sideways, her throat making a hollow, gurgling noise.

"Get up!" the woman with the ax helped the suited man up and they continued running toward the house.

But James couldn't pry his eyes from the woman on the ground. She was rolling back and forth, her fingers clawing her throat as blood spurted out, creating an ever-growing pool of crimson on the road. The front of her shirt was already entirely drenched in blood.

James had never seen that much blood in person, and he'd sure as hell never seen someone dying right in front of him.

The woman's gurgling turned into occasional "gah" sounds. Her thrashing was becoming weaker, too.

"Hey! Come on!" the woman with the ax was standing inches in front of him.

That refocused James's attention. He cast one final look at the choking woman to see the yellow-uniformed man running right at them. Another scream that came from elsewhere told James that more were on the way.

He hopped inside the house and made way for the two strangers to get inside. The woman practically shoved him out of the way as she slammed the door shut and locked it. James was too taken aback by everything that was going on to protest.

Something heavy pounded into the door. The woman held it braced with her palms, even though there was no need to do that. That door was extremely sturdy. Hard to knock open even with a battering ram.

Something scratched the other side of the door, gently but steadily. Then, a familiar voice came from the other side.

"In. In. In."

It repeated the word for what felt like a hundred times. Then the banging resumed. First, it was only at the door. Then it came from the window as well. Pretty soon, screams cracked in the air from everywhere, surrounding the house and veiling it in a sheet that made the temperature drop by twenty degrees.

Opening the door was a mistake. Now they were all going to die.

The walls joined in on the cacophony of slamming sounds until it felt like the entire house was shrinking in on itself, the walls inching closer to crush James and the two strangers that he dared to help.

Something popped in the distance. Despite the bevy of noises, it was distinct enough to be heard. A gunshot, maybe?

Whatever it was, it made the house go silent.

At least, for a moment.

Then, the screams resumed, but they were drawing away from the house. Minutes that seemed like hours passed before the final vestiges of those animalistic caterwauls stopped entirely, draping the house in penetrating silence once again.

Boris Bacic

DANIEL

Skinner insisted they leave the dead body in the elevator while they try to contact HQ. Daniel was against it until he questioned himself why that was so. It was as if a childish part of him expected the body to be gone the next time he returned to the elevator.

A silly idea, he thought to himself dismissively, until he remembered that the idea of crazed humans going around killing each other violently without any cause was just as outlandish.

"Jam the elevator with the fucker," Skinner said.

Richard and Sharpe dragged the bodybuilder halfway out of the elevator and stepped over his body. The corpse's mouth hung open, the eyes staring directly at Daniel as he made his way out. Daniel's initial assumption had been that the man was in his early thirties. A closer look at his face made him rethink that analysis.

Use of PEDs had a way of changing the facial structure of the person, making men look older than they really were and making women look masculine. The victim on the floor was probably in his early to mid-twenties.

Skinner led the group down to the security room. He barged through the door, spun the chair to face him, and plopped into it before turning toward the computer. He began typing on the keyboard, too fast for someone who looked like they only specialized in shooting a firearm.

The research team stood behind him quietly as they waited for Skinner to do his thing.

Daniel glanced at the monitors above the security guard. Lots of movement on the cameras in sections that they'd locked off earlier. The camera overlooking the reception area showed crazies pounding on the glass. The company really could have at least installed some shutters that could be lowered over the glass.

"Shit," Skinner said.

Shit. That single word was never good, especially not in a situation like this one. Skinner didn't need to go into an explanation as to the kind of trouble they were in. The word was self-explanatory, the timbre at which he'd said it even more so.

The only question was: Could the problem be fixed or not?

"There a problem?" Sharpe asked.

"Connection's spotty, and this fucking thing's ancient. Gonna take a while before I can reach HQ."

"Well, you better make it quick. Who knows how long we'll have power for," Daniel said.

"Do... do we expect to, um, lose power?" Melissa asked, another wave of fear shaking her voice.

You've seen the news, right? he wanted to ask.

The entirety of Witherton was a damn mess. It wasn't a matter of whether the police would get things back in order and take control of the city. It was a matter of waiting until the slaughter was over so that the military could move in for the cleanup and occasional rescue. By the time that happened, most of the city would be dead. Only the smart and patient ones would live to see another day.

So, yeah, power would be cut off at some point, sooner rather than later. The internet was already out, probably to minimize panic. A city-wide power outage was bound to follow.

Daniel smiled at Melissa, choosing not to give her an answer to that question. He didn't want her—or the rest of the team—to panic any more than necessary.

"How long do you think it'll take you to get in touch with them?" Sharpe asked Skinner.

"At this rate? Ten minutes, maybe. But then we still gotta wait for them to come evacuate us. Provided they *can* come rescue us."

"Is there a reason why they shouldn't be able to?" Melissa, ever the inquisitive scaredy-cat, asked.

"If this is something on a bigger scale, the military's probably going to cordon off the city to stop the outbreak from spreading. That means they might stop anyone going in and out even if it's for rescue."

"But they have to let the company come extract us. They can't just leave us to die here, right?"

The guard gave her the silent treatment, which was answer enough.

"The army's already on the move," Sharpe said. "I got an emergency alert message a few hours ago about military checkpoints being set up."

Daniel jerked his head toward Doctor Sharpe. "Is that so? I received no such message."

He pulled out his phone just to make sure. No emergency warnings, and his last message had been from Angela. He'd asked her if she was safe, and she responded with, *I'm okay for now.* An hour later, another message came from her, asking, *Dan, what the hell is going on in this town?*

When this whole mess first started that morning, the first thing Daniel had done was call Angela to tell her to get to safety. He had assumed that the one incident he'd seen on the news would turn into two, then four, then eight, and so on.

He had been right.

As confused as she was, Angela listened to him. At first, she protested because she was concerned with the safety of her daughter, but Daniel assured her that the best course of action was to hide and not leave the town because everybody would have the exact same idea, and Angela would find herself between a rock and a hard place.

She listened, but Daniel wasn't sure anymore if it had been a good idea.

"Does it say in your message where the checkpoints are being set up?" Daniel asked Sharpe.

"Yes." Sharpe told him all the addresses, which Daniel typed into the message and sent to Angela.

Wait until the streets are quiet. Then go to the closest checkpoint, he wrote.

What about you? Angela's response came almost immediately.

Don't worry about me. Just get out of the city. I have a feeling things are going to get a lot worse soon.

It took a whole minute before Angela's reply came. *I don't know what you're up to, but please be careful, Dan. If we're lucky, we'll see each other at one of the checkpoints.*

I highly doubt that, Daniel thought, deciding not to respond to Angela's final message.

He shoved the phone into his pocket and looked up. His eyes fell on Richard, whose pale and sweaty face had been illuminated by the glow of the monitors overlooking the facility. His shoulders slouched, and the collar around his neck was drenched, his neck glistening with sweat.

"The hell's the matter with you?" Daniel asked. "Not feeling good?"

"Yeah," Richard muttered. "Think I'm getting sick."

Sharpe and Daniel exchanged a suspicious glance. There was mutual understanding in that look.

Richard needs to be quarantined, that exchange said.

"It must be the stress getting to you," Daniel lied. "You should go lie down. All the rooms on the floor are unoccupied, apparently."

"Seriously, where did the whole science team go? I swear they were here with us just before this all started," Melissa said.

It *was* strange. One moment, they were on the second floor, testing samples, and in the next, gone, as if they vanished in thin air.

"They might have tried to make a run for it but ended up getting swarmed by those lunatics," Daniel said.

It was the only logical explanation. For all they knew, the science team was reduced to a bunch of mangled corpses interspersed on the floor in one of the sections that the crazies had breached.

Panic. It was an emotion so powerful it could trick the mind into ignoring the fact it was running straight into danger's embrace.

"Go lie down, Richard," Daniel repeated.

Richard nodded absent-mindedly. He turned around and, like a zombie, left the security room. Daniel followed his colleague with his gaze until he was out of sight. He waited a while longer before putting a hand on Skinner's shoulder and leaning closer to his ear.

"Keep an eye on Richard," Daniel said. "I think there's something wrong with him."

BEN

"Hello?" Stephanie called out at the counter.

Ben looked around the pharmacy. Intact, but no one was in sight. He kept glancing out into the street, part of him expecting to see that man from the traffic suddenly appear.

"Dammit, where the hell is everyone? Hello? Is anybody here?" Stephanie leaned on the counter and peeked into the backroom.

"I don't think anyone is here, Steph. We should leave," Ben said.

A growing sense of dread skittered across his spine. With each passing second, it grew—so much so that Ben found himself looking left and right just to make sure they weren't being watched.

"Hello? We just need some meds, and we'll be on our way!" Stephanie called out again, ignoring Ben's last remark.

"Stephanie…"

Then Ben's eyes fell on something on the floor in the corner of the room. He stared at it for a long moment because his brain refused to process what it was. Ben blinked, and then the image crystalized, the mind finally accepting reality.

An arm poked from behind the aisle near the corner of the pharmacy. The hand lay upturned on the floor. The fingers were half-closed. Blood caked the nails and streaked along the palmar flexion creases.

Ben had been wrong. The pharmacy hadn't been untouched. Something bad had happened here.

The fingers of the bloodied hand twitched ever so slightly. Ben blinked, trying to convince himself that it was just his imagination, but then it happened again. The hand rotated slowly, merely a ghost of a movement that had Ben questioning whether he was really seeing that.

All at once, the car they'd parked across the street seemed miles distant.

The palm pressed against the floor, revealing bulging, blue veins on the back of the hand. The fingers then contracted, and the hand retreated behind the aisle, out of sight.

"Stephanie, I think we need to leave. Right n—"

When Ben turned, Stephanie was still staring at the backroom. Only now, someone was standing there, in the middle of the dark room, obscured by the shadows.

"Uh, hello?" Stephanie called out softly this time, the vigor drained from her voice.

A loud crash came from the corner of the room. One of the standing shelves had toppled, spilling all the medication on the floor.

"Jesus!" Ben shouted.

Silence. And then something under the crashed shelf caused it to move, merely an inch of a hop before plummeting back to the floor. Stephanie screamed.

Ben looked back at the backroom to see the silhouette from before stepping into view. Stepping was not really the right word. Shuffling was more accurate.

The man in front of them was maybe in his forties, bald, and wearing a lab coat. One shoulder hung lower than the other, and one foot was dragging behind the other. His mouth was agape, jaw and facial features slack as his eyes focused on the customers.

"Stephanie!" Ben called out.

But Stephanie was in a trance. The pharmacy employee stopped shuffling forward and blankly gawked at Stephanie. There was a moment of nothingness in the room as everyone waited with bated breath to see what would happen next.

The toppled shelf rumbled, more violently than before. On cue, the pharmacy employee's mouth closed; then his lips pulled back into a snarl. The contours of his face became rigid, and his bloodshot eyes—how hadn't Ben noticed that before?—gazed at Stephanie with a lust and hunger that could not be put into words.

The crashed shelf continued rattling until the same hand from before was poking out again, this time clawing at the floor, desperate to get out.

Ben spun and bolted toward the door, not caring about standing there a moment longer to try to convince Stephanie they had to leave. He heard her scream as he burst through the door and out into the street.

More shrill screams came from the pharmacy, but they were not Stephanie's. And then more came from the street itself. Ben watched as something a few buildings down fell off the roof and crashed to the ground with a loud thud.

Oh, fuck.

It was a woman, he realized when he looked at her mangled body. Every bone in her body must have been fractured.

Ben raced across the street, jerked open the car door, and fell inside. He slammed it shut and—

"Ben!" Stephanie shouted from across the street.

Ben's finger hovered above the button to lock all the doors. He stopped himself and looked toward the pharmacy. Stephanie was at the entrance, the bald pharmacy employee behind her, pulling her by the back of her shirt.

She broke free of his grip so violently that she fell headlong on the ground. The hem of her shirt that the pharmacy employee had been holding was torn, revealing the rear of her bra and exposed back.

Stephanie planted her palms on the ground and propelled herself onto her feet. Ben's finger continued hovering on the lock button. The pharmacy employee broke into a dash after Stephanie.

Everything seemed to play out in slow motion: Stephanie's tear-stricken and terrified face as she ran across the street toward the car; the pharmacy guy mere feet behind her, running with his hands outstretched forward, his mouth open in a guttural scream, red eyes wide and bulging.

And then, behind him, at the entrance of the pharmacy appeared another person dashing out into the street. The veiny hand with the blood caking it confirmed it was the one that had been stuck under the shelf.

Stephanie wasn't going to make it. Ben knew that much, and he had to make a decision right then. If he allowed her to get inside, the crazy people would simply open the doors and yank them out.

As difficult as it was, Ben pressed the button to lock the doors.

Four simultaneous clicks came from every door just as Stephanie collided with the car. She tried opening the backdoor, but it wouldn't budge.

"Ben!" She pounded on the glass.

It was all she had time to do because, in the next moment, the pharmacy employee collided with her so violently that her forehead slammed against the window. For a split second, Stephanie's eyes rolled to the back of her head as if she was about to lose consciousness.

The man grabbed fistfuls of Stephanie's hair and pulled. That seemed to sober her up. She elbowed the man and held onto her hair as she tried to yank free of his grip.

"Help me!" she screamed at Ben, but there was nothing he could do.

The other man from the pharmacy had caught up to them at last. Ben could see from here it was a guy in his early twenties with a buzz-cut and tattooed forearms. Just like the pharmacy employee, his eyes were bloodshot, and his face contorted into a grimace of hate and hunger.

He collided with Stephanie from behind, causing her to crash into the car's door. The vehicle shook from the impact. He wrapped his arms around her neck from behind while the other person still held her by the hair and now one arm.

Stephanie pressed her palms against the glass on Ben's side of the seat. Ben had never seen such unfiltered fear on someone's face as he did then on Stephanie's. Their eyes met, and if there ever was a plea for help without uttering the words, it was then. But Ben refused to unlock the door. It was too late.

"Ben!" Stephanie shouted as the two men pulled her to the ground.

Stephanie's palm slid down the glass with a squeak as the men pulled her from the car. Only the pharmacy employee remained in view, and he was bent down, doing something to Stephanie as she screamed a blood-curdling scream that hurt Ben's eardrums.

Too late for her. He had to use the moment to get away while he still could.

Ben reached for the key in the ignition. It wasn't there. His heart skipped a beat at the realization that Stephanie still had it on her and that he was going to be stuck in this car.

When he fumbled for the ignition a second time, he felt the key in place, which caused a wave of intense relief to wash over him. He turned it. The engine whirred to life.

Ben thought he could hear Stephanie calling out his name between screams of pain. Ignoring them, he took the steering wheel into his hands and pressed his foot against the gas pedal. The car lurched forward, leaving Stephanie's screaming to fade behind.

Holy fuck, holy fuck, holy fuck, he kept chanting in his mind, in disbelief over what he'd just done.

I left her to die there. Shit. She's dead because of me.

No. Maybe she escaped. Maybe she's still okay.

Only when he was a good distance away, he slowed the car down and looked in the rearview mirror at the place where Stephanie had been attacked. They were still there, the two men, on top of her, kneeling or hunched over, he couldn't tell, doing… something. It was too far away to discern any details.

Except for a few.

Stephanie's hand was splayed on the ground, similar to what Ben had seen back inside the pharmacy. And the men who had attacked her? Their faces and hands had hints of red on them.

PIERCE

It was too quiet. It was as if the city went silent the moment Pierce and his team descended into it, like guests trying to surprise the birthday person.

Pierce didn't like it. From his experience, if a hot zone was too calm, something was wrong. Either an ambush or some other kinds of traps were being prepared.

These enemies weren't smart, though. That's what the general had said, at least. They were an entirely different kind, though, one Pierce had never faced before. It wouldn't be your standard "shoot from the cover and hope you don't get your head blown off" fight.

These enemies would attack blindly even if the odds were against them. And they wouldn't stop until they were dead.

"Nice place," Lincoln said, looking up at the broken windows of the buildings above them. "Might take my next leave here."

"Shut it, Linc," Reynolds commanded. "You'll attract unwanted attention."

They were advancing slowly through the streets, making their way around the piles of dead bodies. By then, Pierce's sense of smell was already so used to the death that surrounded him that he couldn't smell a thing.

"Come on. How hard could it be taking down brainless zombies?" Lincoln asked.

"Wait 'till you get swarmed, and you'll see," Shepherd said.

They stuck to the side of the street to remain less visible. The screams that Pierce thought he'd heard earlier were more prominent now. They intermittently punctuated the air from all directions, and they were close enough for Pierce to discern the story that each scream told.

Mothers watching their kids torn apart by the infected, victims screaming in terror for mercy as a pack chased them down and mauled them to death, dying people's last, feeble gasps as the life drained out of them.

If one listened closely enough, they'd hear words in those screams. Pierce had heard enough of them to understand their language.

Aside from the screams, crashing and gunshots permeated the air. Witherton was a dead city, but the nerves were still spasming and kicking. It was good because Alpha Team could use it to their advantage. The more the infected had their attention elsewhere, the higher Alpha's chances of success would be.

As they progressed, the streets of Witherton grew more cluttered with chains of crashed and abandoned cars while the corpses thinned out. Alpha slowed down because any one of those cars could have been a jack-in-a-box type of trap ready to spring an infected out at them.

Pierce's gaze fell on Amore nightclub across the road.

Church Street, Pierce remembered. He hadn't often gone down this road while living in Witherton because it was out of the way to anything, and it only had an occasional club, seedy motel, or questionable fast-food place to lure unsuspecting outsiders.

The team made good progress down the street without encountering any signs of hostiles, but then Reynolds raised a hand to signal the team to stop. Pierce held his breath as he squinted at the street ahead. That was when he saw it.

Movement as a silhouette slunk behind an overturned van.

"Hostiles ahead," Reynolds said. "Follow me."

He hurriedly stepped inside the closest alley, giving Pierce enough time to see it wasn't just one hostile ahead. It was a whole mob of them mingling in the middle of the street like drugged-out ravers.

The team followed Reynolds as he jogged to the end of the alley. He peeked out into the street then pulled back.

"Shit. More of them," he said and then eyed the alley up and down. "There." He pointed. "Let's get on top of this building and scout for a way forward."

"On it," Lincoln said as he approached the closest door.

He rattled the doorknob then stepped back and kicked the door down. It was too loud against the stillness of the air, but hopefully, the infected weren't that good at pinpointing noise.

Murphy provided cover while Shepherd disappeared inside. Others soon followed. They climbed the stairs and emerged on the rooftop.

"Looks like someone's been waiting for this all their life," Lincoln said.

Pierce needed a moment to understand what he meant, and then he beheld the corpse of the man propped up against the parapet wall in a sitting position. His lower jaw was gone, the front of his flannel shirt soaked with blood. One of his eyes was missing.

A sniper rifle lay next to him, ammo from an overturned box spilled on the floor.

"This guy must have picked them off from here," Murphy said. "But why?"

"Why the fuck not?" Lincoln asked. "For fun."

Meanwhile, Reynolds and Pierce walked up to the edge and observed the street. The building they stood on was only five floors high, so they couldn't get a good look, but the view of the crowd that surrounded the adjacent streets left them boggled their minds about how they would proceed.

"Damn," Reynolds said. "No way through."

Pierce walked a lap around the wall, checking each street below.

"I see some civilians," Lincoln said.

No one had noticed until then that Lincoln was looking through the scope of the sniper.

"You sure they're not hostiles?" Shepherd asked.

"Pretty sure," Lincoln said. "Three men and a woman. She looks thick. That's it, baby. Turn around so I can see that ass. Goddamn, she's packing."

"Forget the civilians. Do you see a way out?" Reynolds asked.

"Nothing. The place is crawling with those zombies."

Pierce scanned the general direction Lincoln was facing, but he couldn't locate the group he was talking about. "What are the civilians doing?"

"Sneaking through the streets. I could shoot one of them in the leg from here, captain. Have the undead turn their attention to them and give us a clear passage."

"Are you out of your mind? Those are civilians. We don't kill them," Pierce interjected.

"Not unless they're a threat."

"Those people aren't a threat," Shepherd came to Pierce's support.

"Maybe. But they can help us with our mission." Lincoln shrugged. "Besides, not like they're going to make it out of here."

Pierce could see Lincoln's finger sliding over the trigger, ready to squeeze it.

"Think you can make the shot from here?" Reynolds asked.

Pierce clenched his jaw. If the captain approved of that, then Pierce and Shepherd's words would mean nothing even if Murphy decided to grow a pair and back them up.

To Reynolds, the mission was always the most important thing even if it meant throwing a few lives away. Pierce knew how the captain's mind worked: They could use the civilians as live bait now, or they could let them die in vain later.

That was how Lincoln saw it, too. While they were on the mission, civilians weren't people. They were a tool to help the team complete their objectives.

"You're making a mistake, captain," Pierce said, choosing to try to reason with Reynolds rather than Lincoln.

Reynolds's eyes briefly flitted in Pierce's direction then back at Lincoln. "Linc?"

"Yeah, I can make the shot."

Pierce needed to think fast. If he didn't, innocent people would get killed. Sure, the chances civilians had of making it out of the city alive were close to zero, but at least that blood wouldn't be on Alpha's hands.

"There's no need to do that. There's another way out," Pierce rapidly recited.

Reynolds turned to fully face Pierce with an expectant look on his face. "Where?"

"Come over here." Pierce motioned for the captain to follow him to the edge of the roof. "There." He pointed below at the street, at a set of subway-style stairs leading underground.

Shepherd, Reynolds, and Murphy were leaning over the edge to see what Pierce was pointing at.

"There's an underground mall over there," Pierce said. "It'll take us out right over... there." He pointed to a similar set of stairs far behind the convergence of infected. "We'll give the infected the slip without them ever knowing about us."

Reynolds stared down at the set of stairs, a pensive frown plastered to his face as if he was contemplating whether to go with Pierce's or Lincoln's method.

"It's definitely a safer method," Shepherd said. "Shots from a sniper could draw them to us instead."

"Looks good to me. Nice going, Pierce." Reynolds finally said, his hand falling on Pierce's shoulder in passing. "Move it, people."

"Captain…" Lincoln started.

"On your feet, Lincoln," Reynolds interrupted.

Lincoln looked through the scope again. "I can still make the shot. They're still in sight. Just give me the green light and—"

"That's enough, Lincoln. How many times do I need to tell you to stop fucking around? Drop the sniper and let's move," Reynolds said, his voice sterner than usual.

To Pierce's surprise and relief, Lincoln complied without any sardonic remarks. The tension that hung in the air up until that moment dispersed like shards of a broken vase.

"Your bleeding hearts are gonna jeopardize the mission," Lincoln said as he stood, shooting scornful looks at Shepherd and Pierce.

For someone who joked all the time, Lincoln sure could get gravely serious.

Pierce looked at Shepherd. She smiled. He smiled back, a gesture that silently said, "Thanks for having my back."

Then the team was descending the stairs back out into the jaws of the beast.

Boris Bacic

KRISTA

Krista had spent the entire night tossing and turning, dreading the arrival of morning. She and Eric had gone to bed late because they had to decide what he was going to pack.

A knot that had tightened inside her stomach refused to abate throughout the entire night. A few times, she wanted to shake Eric awake and tell him that she changed her mind and she didn't want to let him go.

But it had to be done, for Nelson.

Without help, he would only get worse.

Initially, though, Krista had tried dissuading Eric from going out there.

"But what are you going to do out there?" she had asked him after he suggested going outside.

"I told you, I'm going to look for help," he had said. "A doctor for Nelson."

"Eric, we watched the news together. You know what's out there. It's not safe. You said it yourself. Joe is…"

She couldn't find the right word to describe their neighbor.

Dangerous? Crazy? Violent?

None of those words fit the description of Joe, and yet, that was what he was like. It felt so surreal to not have contact with anyone in Witherton. Krista wondered if all of their family and friends who lived in the city were in Joe's state.

More importantly, what was causing that? It was too abrupt and too inexplicable.

That was, perhaps, what worried Krista the most. If they had at least been informed by the government or the

CDC about what this was and how to combat it, Krista would have had some peace of mind. However, as it stood, she felt like she was fighting an invisible enemy.

"I'm going to find help. I promise." Eric's words held no weight to them, only the certain worry that had penetrated Krista's bones since this all started.

They didn't speak after that at all that night.

In the morning, Eric's alarm on the phone blared on the nightstand until he blindly located it and shut the damn thing off. Krista was wide awake and had been for at least an hour before that.

"I'll make you some breakfast," she said atonally as she threw off the blanket.

It was alarmingly cold, but it hardly bothered her compared to the thoughts running like a tornado through her head. She went upstairs to check on Nelson. He was still out, still burning, but he spoke more often— disconnected words that made no sense.

Krista had held onto the hope that it meant Nelson was getting better, but the fever that refused to leave his body told her otherwise.

If anything, it helped her feel less despondent about Eric leaving.

"Just hold on, baby. Daddy's going to get help," she said as she kissed his blazing forehead.

She fried some eggs and bacon for Eric and packed sandwiches and non-perishable food for him.

"How is he?" he asked as he ate by the kitchen table.

"Bad. He's not getting any better."

"All the more reason for me to go."

The entire time, Krista was leaning on the counter with her arms crossed, staring intently at her husband, regretting not admiring that handsome face more often. Gawking at him while he ate before his trip, she felt like studying an hour before the test.

It was as ineffective. Crammed information mixed with the anxiety before the test caused no retention of what she should have memorized.

Similarly, staring at Eric as he sat at the kitchen table made her feel no sense of comfort or love that she so desperately tried to siphon in these last moments, something to hold on to for as long as possible. The only thing she felt was worry and sadness.

Noticing her distress, he put the fork down, pushed the chair out, and walked up to her.

"Babe, what's got you so worried? Hmm?" he asked as he caressed her cheek with the back of his hand.

That you won't come back. That it'll be all up to me to save Nelson. That I won't know what to do without your guidance. That this is goodbye.

She couldn't tell him any of those things, though. She didn't want to jumble up his head just before his trip. He needed to think clearly while out there. Otherwise, he would die.

He would die.

That was the first time Krista understood what Eric's departure meant. It made her chest constrict as if her lungs were imploding on themselves, pressing all air out of her.

"Everything out there. I think Witherton is too dangerous right now," she said, hoping he would settle for that.

"I know. I'll be careful." He nodded.

"Avoid crowded areas, please," she said.

"I will."

They held hands and then kissed for a very long moment. Parting her lips from his, Krista trembled. It was time. She knew that much, and his face said so, too.

"I have to go," he confirmed.

Please, don't go. Don't leave me and Nelson alone.

"Right." She nodded without a complaint. "I put your backpack in the foyer."

"I'm gonna go say bye to Nelson before I go," he said.

They went up to Nelson's room. Eric slowly opened the door so as not to disturb Nelson's sleep, even though he slept most of the time these days.

"Hey, buddy. You awake?" Eric whispered.

No response other than the soft inhaling and exhaling.

Eric walked up to the bed and sat at the edge. Nelson gave no indication that he was aware of his dad's presence. Eric inhaled through his nose and took Nelson's hand.

"Listen, I'm going to need to leave for a while. I'm going to find someone to make you better, okay?" Eric said. "I need you to look after your mom while I'm gone, okay?"

He paused, and Krista sensed his voice was on the verge of breaking.

"I don't know how long I'll be, but when I'm back, we can go back to practicing your pitching, okay?"

He audibly swallowed. He sounded like he wanted to say something more but was trying really hard not to break down. Maybe an *I love you, son,* but Eric was never a person who expressed emotions. Even toward Krista, saying *I love you was a rare occurrence.* When he said it, Krista would know he really meant it.

Eric stood from the bed. As he started toward the door, Nelson's head turned, and a word escaped his mouth.

"Dad..." he said.

A moment of hopefulness swaddled Krista. Had it not been a life-or-death scenario, Krista would have been jealous that Nelson was more responsive to his dad than his mom.

Eric spun to face his son, but Nelson was already asleep again.

***

Standing in the foyer, Krista felt probably the way Eric felt in the room with Nelson—trying to maintain her composure.

"Please stay out of sight. And drink plenty of water," Krista said.

Eric smiled, the kind of smile he'd give Krista whenever he felt a surge of affection toward her.

"I will." He took Krista's hands into his. "Take care of Nelson while I'm gone."

"How long do you think you'll be gone?"

She realized how much that sounded like something Nelson should have asked instead of her, but she was too distressed to worry whether her questions were infantile.

"I don't know." He shook his head. "But if I'm not back in five days… you'll have to do whatever's necessary to keep Nelson safe."

Tears blurred Krista's vision. She felt that it was okay to cry at that moment.

"But what if I can't? What if I don't know what to do?"

He gave her a reassuring smile. "You will. You always do. It's going to be hard, but I believe in you, Kris. I still stand behind what I've been telling you all these years. I see something in you that you don't. That's why I'm not worried about you and Nelson at all."

Krista suppressed a sob as Eric planted a kiss on her lips. He smelled like vanilla. She never knew what products he used to smell that way, but she loved that about him.

"I love you, baby," he said, and it only made Krista want to cry even more.

"I love you, too," she said.

They hugged tightly, and then, he was through the door. He cast one final look in her direction and forced a smile before Krista closed the door.

That was when she finally allowed herself to break down into ugly, loud sobs.

It was the last time she'd ever see her husband alive.

BEN

Ben parked Stephanie's car in the driveway and turned the key in the ignition. The engine sputtered out of life, leaving Ben in a silence that caused his ears to start buzzing.

His hands trembled on the steering wheel. Whenever he closed his eyes, even for a blink, he could see Stephanie getting torn apart by those... things.

That's what they were. Things. Monsters. Not people. No humans could behave that way. What in the hell had happened to them?

There had been madness in their eyes, Ben remembered. Hunger, hate, and some other things so primordial their verbal descriptions fell into oblivion. But he understood well what it was, no matter how impossible it was to put into words.

It was like communicating with a predatorial animal and knowing exactly how dangerous it was because of its rigid body language, the teeth it was showing, and the focus in its eyes.

Something is fucking wrong with this city. What the fuck is happening? Why isn't the government doing anything?

Ben stepped out of the car, not bothering to close the door. If someone wanted to take this shit car, he couldn't care. Not only was it a cheap piece of garbage, but it was scratched to kingdom come. He was glad it was Stephanie's car, and not his.

He fished the keys to his house out of his pocket and unlocked the front door. After stepping inside, he turned on the alarm systems and walked into the kitchen. He needed a drink, badly.

He traced a finger along the array of bottles neatly lined on the shelf above the counter and chose a Laphroaig, price be screwed. He could have sold it for a ton of money because of its age, but Ben didn't care about earning money from selling alcoholic beverages.

Ben bought the Laphroaig for a little over $2000. It was the most expensive drink he'd paid for. His insurance company paid him more than a hefty salary, so it was no problem.

Melissa had been against it, but Ben was adamant about starting a whiskey collection. She couldn't possibly understand. She hadn't tasted anything stronger than beer in her life. Appreciating whiskey took a lot of class.

He opened the cabinet that held the glasses, took one out, and placed it on the counter. He retrieved two ice cubes from the freezer and tossed them inside the glass. They clinked and whirled before coming to a halt.

Uncapping the bottle of the Laphroaig, Ben brought it closer to his nose and allowed the aroma to infiltrate his nostrils. The strong redolence wiggled deep into his sinuses, so much that he could almost taste the scotch in his mouth.

He tipped the bottle's neck toward the glass and poured the brown liquid inside, enough to get the ice cubes off the bottom of the glass. He placed the bottle on the counter, took the glass into his hand, and strolled into the living room.

"Alexa, turn on TV," he said.

The middle ridge of the cube-like device glowed with a blue color.

"Okay," the robotic voice said.

The black screen of the TV mounted above the electric fireplace powered on. Instead of the usual action or drama taking place on the screen, Ben's view was met with a static image with the message "EMERGENCY

BROADCAST" over it. With it came a voice booming against the silence of the house.

"…your homes. Lock your doors, cover your windows, and avoid making too much noise. Do not go outside under any circumstances. You will receive further instructions soon."

Then silence.

"What the hell?" Ben asked as he spun the glass in his hand in small circles, making the brown liquid slosh around and the ice cubes waltz around each other.

Then the voice started again, "This is an emergency government broadcast for the citizens of Witherton. Stay inside your homes. Lock your doors, cover your windows, and avoid making too much noise. Do not go outside under any circumstances. You will receive further instructions soon."

Ben downed the drink in his hand with two big gulps, not bothering to savor the ancient taste. He then slammed the glass with the ice cubes onto the coffee table and pinched his nose, listening to the message on the TV.

This was no longer just a passing news article. It was real, and it was dangerous. Life-threatening, apparently. Ben had to defend himself. Dammit, why did he listen to Melissa and not get a gun? She had been against having a firearm in their home, quoting something about the chances of shooting a loved one rather than the intruder.

More than ever before, Ben felt angry with her. If he had a gun, he would have felt a lot safer. Hell, he would have been able to go out there and rescue her.

But like this? Unarmed?

Welco Labs was all the way on the other side of the town. He would be willing to meet Melissa halfway there, but going all the way to the company? After everything he'd seen? After Stephanie got killed right in front of his eyes? Without a gun on top of that?

He'd hate to say it, but it was probably every person for themselves. Melissa was on her own. But if she was at Welco Labs, she should be safe, right? That place was tightly secure, and nothing could get past it.

Ben took his phone out of his pocket and checked for notifications. Nada. He tried sending a message and calling Melissa. No luck.

He was about to put his phone into his pocket when he received a text message. His heart leaped into his throat, bringing with it a need for another glass of scotch. Until he realized that the message was actually an emergency alert from the government, echoing what the TV man was saying.

"Alexa, turn off TV," Ben said.

"Okay," Alexa said, the blue lines along the middle of the devices pulsating for a moment.

The screen of the TV went black, muting the voice of the announcer. Ben sat on the couch and stared at the coffee table. The ice cubes sat in a shallow layer of water at the bottom of the glass. Ben regretted quaffing the scotch so quickly without allowing himself a moment to savor the taste.

He needed another glass, but he couldn't afford it. He had to keep a cool head. The day was only just beginning, apparently, even though it was already four p.m. The question was, what was he supposed to do?

The emergency broadcast said that staying inside was the best course of action, but that was the government, and they were known to fuck up every now and again. Ben's house was relatively safe, yes, but it wasn't designed to withstand whatever was happening out there.

If those crazy people appeared in the neighborhood, how long would it take until they stormed the house? Alarms he set in place earlier were clearly useless, except to maybe scare off looters. The police weren't going to come because they would be much too busy.

Ben climbed to the bedroom and peeked toward the neighbor's house across the street. Streaks of orange snaked along the sky, eating away any remaining vestiges of blue. It would be night soon.

No movement there or in the street itself. He wondered if the neighbors were still at work—or worse. He wondered if those crazy people were in the neighborhood, too.

Broadside was considered one of the fanciest and most expensive neighborhoods in Witherton. Crime rates were close to zero, and everybody knew everybody. Ben didn't like the neighbors that much because they acted like pretentious pricks since most of them were either successful business owners or worked for big companies.

Ben and Melissa were considered to be in the lowest tier of Broadside, and he could sense the alienation coming from the other families in the neighborhood. It didn't bother him. They were annoying to hang out with, anyway.

Melissa seemed offended by it, though. She tried hard to become friends with the other women, but apparently, that didn't matter to them. If you were poor, or at least what they considered poor, you weren't welcome.

In any other neighborhood, Melissa and Ben's combined paycheck of quarter-six figures would have them hailed as royalty. In Broadside, they were bugs squashed on the underside of somebody's shoe.

Fuck them. I hope they all died today, Ben found himself thinking, remorselessly.

He could just imagine them panicking while stuck in traffic like he was earlier. Their money or position in the world couldn't bail them out if one of those crazy people went after them. They'd become just another corpse on the pile.

His thoughts had trailed. The original question that hovered above his head was whether Broadside would be safe from the calamity that plagued the rest of Witherton. If this thing, whatever it was, spread wide enough, then even Broadside wouldn't be safe.

So long wine parties, book club meetups, and gossiping at barbecues. And good riddance, if that happened.

Focus, Ben. What to do?

He never was the type to sit on his ass and wait for rescue—if rescue even came. So, finding a way out of the city was the next best solution.

His eyes fell on the framed picture on the wall.

But what about Melissa?

The picture was of him and his wife on the day they first moved into their new house. They were hugging in a way that Melissa had been smiling. It was Ben's coworker who had come to help them move in who took that picture. Melissa liked the captured moment so much that she had it framed and hung on the wall.

A pang of guilt washed over Ben. He and Melissa had been together for years. One incident in the city and the invisible umbilical cord that bound them together was severed, perhaps permanently. The right thing to do would be to look for her, he knew that much.

But Melissa was all the way on the other side of the city. There was no way he could reach her. Maybe when this all blew over, he could look for her, but it was too dangerous to do so while the chaos lasted.

So, what then?

Ben scratched his forehead. He shouldn't have even been thinking about this. She was his wife. Going after her was morally the only right thing to do.

He hated to admit it, but he was being selfish. Melissa was his *wife*. He was supposed to care about her. He'd heard of people throwing themselves in danger's way to save their spouses; of people searching for their missing loved ones for years, unable to go on with their lives…

But he wasn't that kind of a husband. A protective instinct toward Melissa had never been there.

No, that wasn't true. It was there but only when it came to protecting her just as he would protect anything that belonged to him.

But protecting all of his property was no longer an option. He would lose some things irrevocably, that was a fact. He just needed to figure out what was dead weight that he could cut loose. He didn't like where his thoughts drifted when the term "dead weight" came to his mind.

In the end, this wasn't a movie. It was not about heroism. It was about survival.

And the first rule of survival was prioritizing your own life.

Boris Bacic

HEATHER

Heather was glad she hadn't thrown out Abby's old school bag. The straps were split and tattered and tied back together. It had been a way to make the school bag functional until Heather's paycheck, which was when she bought Abby the new bag.

She packed essentials into both school bags, but she also put the dinosaur puzzle into Abby's because she knew that thing would calm her down if worse came to worst.

Heather hated that stupid puzzle. She hated how she memorized where each piece went, and she despised the stupid T-Rex standing menacingly with its jaw unhinged, the brontosaurus behind him eating grass, and the pterodactyl flying in the sky as if the three lived in a perfect, peaceful union.

"Why do we have to go, Sis?" Abby asked.

"Because," Heather replied curtly while zipping up the school bag.

"Why?"

"Because I said so."

"I don't wanna leave. I like it here."

The apartment was a dump. The building was a haven for crackheads. But for Abby, it was home. Of course she wouldn't want to leave the place she was so comfortable in.

For a split second, Heather pondered what it would have been like to leave Abby at home while she went in search of the military checkpoint. An enticing thought but ultimately one that wasn't doable.

Their parents made it clear—if something were to happen to them, Heather was to take care of Abby. The more time Heather spent with Abby, though, the less she wanted to honor that final wish.

She's your sister. Stop being so mean.

Just like always, a nibble of regret slithered into her chest. She wasn't supposed to be feeling this way toward Abby, and yet, it was becoming harder and harder to ignore those thoughts.

She stared at Abby zipping up her school bag, and she felt nothing short of resentment toward her sister. All oblivious to how she ruined Heather's life, oblivious to pretty much everything except her own little bubble.

But then Abby looked at Heather and smiled with a gaze full of love and admiration that she so clearly displayed toward her big sister. The way the two of them looked at each other differed like the ground and the sky. Abby wasn't aware of Heather's feelings toward her, and that made another wave of guilt crash into Heather.

"Are you ready to go?" she asked.

"Yes, Sis." Abby hoisted the school bag on and stood.

"Do you need to use the bathroom?"

"No."

"Are you sure?" Heather raised an eyebrow. "We won't be able to stop on the way, so you better go now if you need to."

Abby looked into empty space as she pondered Heather's suggestion, finally sliding the straps off her shoulders and allowing the bag to plop to the floor.

"Okay," she said in a despondent voice as she waltzed into the bathroom.

Heather sat on the couch next to the charging phone. She unlocked it, only to be greeted by zero notifications. Without the internet, it was pretty much a brick. Heather hadn't realized how addicted she was to the device until this all started happening.

She'd pull it out every now and again, just to check for notifications on the many social media apps she had installed. She even swore she thought she heard her phone buzzing or ringing, only to unlock it and see nothing on it. But that was the thing. She could simply pull it out and check it, and if nothing was there, it went back into her pocket.

The inability to do that was exasperating. It was bad enough that she couldn't check social media, but with the entire internet out, she felt cut off from the rest of the world.

She had tried calling the emergency services the day before, but even that wasn't working. Messages didn't go through, either. Maybe the internet was out just for the neighborhood. It was Baldwin River, after all. Maybe some maniac climbed on top of the internet provider building and tore off the antenna or something.

Heather hoped she'd get some reception once they reached a different part of town.

The sound of flushing came from the bathroom. The door opened, and Abby stepped outside. "I'm ready, Sis."

Heather stuffed the phone in her pocket and packed the charger into her school bag. They might run into places where she could charge her phone, right?

Who knew? Maybe St. Peter wouldn't even be bad. Really, getting out of Baldwin was the only thing that worried Heather. From there, it would be a home stretch to the military checkpoint. Plus, they'd be in the car. They could just lock it and drive away if things went south.

"Put your school bag on," Heather said.

Abby did as she was told. Heather knelt in front of Abby and gently put her hands on her arms. "Abby, listen. When we're outside, I need you to stay close to me at all times, okay?"

Abby nodded.

"Say it." Heather gently shook her.

"You need me to stay close to you at all times," Abby repeated.

"Good girl."

"Where are we going, Sis?"

Heather thought for a moment. "It's... a surprise."

"What kind of surprise?"

"If I told you, it wouldn't be a surprise anymore, would it?"

"But I wanna know!"

Heather couldn't engage in a discussion with Abby about what the surprise in question was. If she did, Abby would start throwing a tantrum. So, what she did instead was divert Abby's attention.

"Abby, this is very important. We're going to have to be extremely quiet when we're outside, okay?"

"Are we playing a game?"

"Yes. We're playing a game."

"Yay!" Abby hopped. "What's the name of the game?"

"It's, uh... it's called the Sneaking Game."

"The Sneaking Game?"

"Yes. It means we have to be as quiet as possible and sneak through the streets without being seen by other people. If we get caught, we lose the game."

"What if we just get seen and not caught?"

Heather bit her lip. "We get negative points. And if we get enough negative points, we... we won't get the reward at the end of the game."

"What's the reward? What's the reward?" Abby bounced up and down.

Heather shrugged. "Guess you'll have to sneak quietly to find out."

Abby broke free of Heather's arms and ran into the foyer. "Then what are we waiting for? Come on, Sis, we have to win the game!"

Heather was glad convincing Abby went so smoothly. She just hoped her enthusiasm for the fake game would last them to the military checkpoint.

Boris Bacic

JAMES

"Jesus. Jesus," the suited man said, his wheezy breaths too loud against the oppressive quiet in the room.

James beheld the two strangers in his house in detail only then for the first time. The man had short, grizzled hair. The strands clung to his skull. His neatly trimmed beard was mostly white with a few brown hairs sticking out. Despite the messy and dirty suit, James could tell that the man was well-standing. Might have been a salesman or a lawyer, based on the way he dressed.

The woman's hair was curly, but it was tied into a bun so tightly that it almost looked straight in places. Her blouse and jeans told nothing about her. If anything, the ax in her hand dripping with blood said more about her.

Truthfully, the way she killed that woman out there by whacking her in the throat with an ax told a lot more about her than her clothing did.

One thing was for sure, though. The ax, the backpack, the tightly bound hair, the clothes that allowed for good mobility—all of it said that she was prepared for this. Whether she was waiting for something like this to happen or just adapted very quickly was still questionable.

"Quiet." The woman raised a hand, instantly silencing the suited man's breathing.

That caused James's breathing to halt, too.

She let her hand drop after a while and said, "Okay. It looks like they're gone for the moment. But we need to go. Now."

"Go? Where?" James asked.

"Anywhere but here," the woman said. "As soon as they're done playing with whatever caught their attention, they'll come back here. We need to leave before that happens."

"But where are we supposed to—"

"Pack the essentials. You'll probably need some food and water." The woman brushed past James and was scanning the living room, the ax held tightly in her hands, poised to attack the next person who dared come at her.

"Is anyone here with you?" she asked as she peeked into the kitchen.

Before James could give her an answer, she was already striding inside. He didn't like this person strolling around his house like it was hers.

"Hey, hold on. Hold on. Lady…" He followed her into the kitchen.

She snapped at him. For a second, he thought she was going to turn the ax on him. It dawned on James that he was locked inside his house with two strangers, one of them armed with an ax. If they so much as wanted to kill and rob him, they could do so.

It also dawned on him what a stupid idea it was to let people inside when he didn't know a thing about them.

"Angela," the woman said.

It took James a very long moment to understand that she was introducing herself.

"Angela. Okay."

"And that's Travis." She jutted her head over James's shoulder.

James turned around to see the suited man leaning on the doorframe, his arms crossed.

"And, do you have a name?" Angela asked.

"Yeah. I'm James."

"Okay, James. Now that we got the introductions out of the way, can we hurry it along, please?"

"Hurry what along? I helped you out back there, and now you want to return outside?"

"It's not safe here. We have to leave."

"Hold on a minute. The emergency broadcast said that we're supposed to stay put," James said.

"Old broadcast," Travis spoke up. "You didn't receive a new message in the meantime?"

"What new message?"

James pulled out his phone, but he had no other emergency alerts.

"Military checkpoints," Angela said. "The army's organizing an evacuation plan there. That's our best bet."

"I don't understand why I haven't received that message," James said.

Travis shrugged. "Signal might be scrambled. The whole town's gone to hell. Haven't you seen the news?"

"Um… a little bit. What exactly is going on?"

"We'll explain on the way," Angela hopped into the discussion. "For now, grab some supplies, and let's go."

It felt sudden, leaving the house like that. James had no idea how long he'd be absent, how long this situation would last, and how long until things went back to normal. He scooped up a backpack from the closet in his bedroom and stuffed food and water into it.

The food could hardly be called food. Two Snickers bars, one Bounty, and a bag of Doritos. He knew he had at least one can of tuna somewhere, but he didn't have enough time to look for it. The half-full bottle of water would hardly be enough, but it would have to do. He also took his cigs and lighter.

He finally took a kitchen knife and stuffed it into his jeans.

"Okay. Got everything you need?" Angela asked.

"Yeah." James nodded.

"Then let's go. A checkpoint shouldn't be far from here."

James hardly even had time to look at the house when they exited through the backdoor. He bought it barely two years ago. James had always been minimalistic, and he didn't value material things too much. And yet, closing the door behind him, he hadn't realized just how attached he was to the house and the place he called home.

He couldn't shake the feeling that this was the last time he would gaze upon this neighborhood.

THE END

INFECTED CITY

Book 1: Emergency Broadcast
Book 2: Necrotic Streets
Book 3: Quarantine Terror
Book 4: Decaying Haven
Book 5: Outbreak Chaos
Book 6: Dead End

Printed in Great Britain
by Amazon

23862990R00098